make lemonade

Other POINT SIGNATURE
paperbacks you will enjoy:

Local News
by Gary Soto

Orfe
by Cynthia Voigt

Toning the Sweep
by Angela Johnson

PRAISE FOR
VIRGINIA EUWER WOLFF'S
MAKE LEMONADE:

"Wolff's latest novel stretches her considerable talents in a new direction. Written in a riveting, stream-of-consciousness fashion, with the lines laid out on the page as if they were verses of a poem, the book plunges into the depths of inner-city poverty. . . . Rooted not in a particular culture, but in the community of poverty, the story offers a penetrating view of the conditions that foster our ignorance, destroy our self-esteem, and challenge our strength. . . . At once disturbing and uplifting, this finely nuanced, touching portrait proudly affirms our ability to reach beyond ourselves and reach out to one another."

—*Booklist*, starred review

"A spare, beautifully crafted depiction of a 14-year-old whose goal of escaping poverty is challenged by friendship with a single teenage mother. These girls could be from more than one ethnic group and almost any inner city. Powerfully moving."

—*Kirkus Reviews*, pointed review

"The tale is told in natural first-person, and in rhythmic prose arranged in open verse. The poetic form emphasizes the flow of the teenager's language and thought. The form invites readers to drop some preconceptions about novels, and they will find the plot and characters riveting. *Make Lemonade* is a triumphant, outstanding story."

—*School Library Journal*, starred review

"Poetry is everywhere, as Wolff (*The Mozart Season*) proves by fashioning her novel with meltingly lyric blank verse in the voice of an inner-city 14-year-old. . . . Radiant with hope, this keenly observed and poignant novel is a stellar addition to . . . literature."

—*Publishers Weekly*, starred review

"With a plot that develops incredible dramatic momentum, this fast-reading book may appeal to readers just like Jolly. Vague in setting—the story could take place in any inner city—as well as ethnicity, Wolff's characters grab hold and don't let go. The author's fans will celebrate this new book that provides the same emotional reading experience as her earlier novels, *Probably Still Nick Swansen* and *The Mozart Season*. . . ."

—*The Horn Book Magazine*, starred review

"Verna LaVaughn ·is only 14, but she needs money—to help sustain herself and her mother and for her own college education. She answers an ad ("Babysitter Needed Bad") and finds her employer to be Jolly, a 17-year-old mother of two toddlers ("leaking liquids everywhere") who has an iffy job and minimal housekeeping skills. Out of life's "lemons," both young women make some lemonade. That lemonade is not, however, cloyingly sweet. By the end of the story, Jolly has not turned into June Cleaver and vanished into the middle class. Wolff's account of how both Verna and Jolly change is moving, and the form she has chosen, arranging the lines more like poetry than prose, creates a feeling of specialness without any hint of preciosity."

—*Chicago Tribune*

POINT•SIGNATURE

make lemonade

Virginia Euwer Wolff

SCHOLASTIC INC.
New York Toronto London Auckland Sydney

For young mothers

Thanks to:
Marilyn E. Marlow, Christine Poole-Jones,
Gail Westlin, Anthony Wolff, Juliet Wolff,
Jean Harmon, Joe Croft, Clackamas County
Sheriff's Office, Willamette Falls Hospital,
The Oregon Trail Chapter of the American
Red Cross, Mike Thompson of Buck Medical
Services, Lawson Fusao Inada, Mary Gunesch,
my students at Mt. Hood Academy, Laura Godwin,
George Wen, Brenda Bowen, and to Max Hamel
for his handprints.

ISBN 0-590-48141-X

12 11 10 9 8 7 6 5 4 3   4 5 6 7 8 9/9

Printed in the U.S.A.   01

First Scholastic printing, August 1994

part one

1.

I am telling you this just the way it went
with all the details I remember as they were,
and including the parts I'm not sure about.
You know, where something happened
but you aren't convinced
you understood it?
Other people would maybe tell it different
but I was there.

It's like a bird. One minute it's picking up something
off the sidewalk
and you recognize it all together as a bird eating.
The next minute it's gone into the traffic on the street
and you try and remember how that bird was,
how its pointy feet were strutting
and its neck was bulging back and forth
but it's gone and you're the only one can tell
it was there in front of you.

This is like that.

2.

*M*e and my friends Myrtle and Annie went to the bulletin board
where the office puts up notes
if they're approved by the school:
So-and-so wants a housecleaner or a painter
or somebody to babysit or be a janitor's assistant.
They give you a number to call,
they put it on 12 little tabs at the bottom
and you pull one off to carry with you to the phone.
My friends went for housecleaning
but I saw this note that said
BABYSITTER NEEDED BAD. It was smudged in the corner
and wrinkled a little bit but you could still read it.
The tabs were still there, all of them hanging in a row.
I pulled off a tab because nobody else had.

I called this babysitting number
and her voice answered
like we could be friends,
right away.

It would be a certain number of hours
she promised.
My Mom says I can work the hours I need to
but always leave time for homework.
Homework is a completely required thing
like a vaccination.

4

You meet my Mom
you'll see what I mean.

So this babysitting job
sounded like a fair arrangement,
I could still do my homework,
and she said her name was Jolly.
"Jolly?" I said to her. I never heard that name before.
"So?" she said.
I told her my name, LaVaughn. She laughed.
"LaVaaaawwwwnnnn," she said.
Then she went back to the babysitting subject.

We said we agreed about the conditions of work
and I'd go to her place right after school
to meet the little ones
who had started to scream behind the phone.

3.

I go to meet this Jolly like she says
at her place. The building was broken-down looking,
it was even a worse place than where we live.
The sidewalk is sticky,
the garbage cans don't have lids, somebody without teeth
was talking to herself in front of the door.

This Jolly's apartment is disorderly and it smells.
But I can see right away there's a lot causing it.
"Jeremy here, he's 2, and this here's Jilly," she says,
jouncing a gooey baby in her arms
and something gurgles out of that one's nose
and Jolly scoots fast past me to the kitchen counter
to pick up a rag
to wipe it with. I look down at Jeremy,
he walks away in that tumbling walk little kids have
and he goes and throws all three stained-brown sofa pillows
off the sofa onto the floor.

This Jolly she looks me up and down and she says
"You don't look like you're beefy enough.
These kids are heavy."
She's referring to my skinniness,
which the gym teachers referred to my whole life.
I tell her I'm stronger than I look.
She looks at me sideways.

She says her other sitter quit for better pay
and I can begin anytime, the sooner the better.
She'll lose her job if she don't go back tomorrow
or the next day.
She works evening shift over at the plant.
She says, "Jeremy, can you say 'LaVaughn'?" down to him
and Jeremy who's barely paying attention says No
and puts his finger on my shoelace, which is red.

I'm standing in their smelly apartment
looking over the way things are going to be,
me with these two small ones that I can already tell
are leaking liquids everywhere.
Jolly turns out to be 17. I could still say No
just as quick as Jeremy did about my name.
Then this Jolly she says, "I can't do it alone no longer,
see, I'll get fired, it's a good job,
I work for the factory, you work for me,
Jilly and Jeremy can count on you being here,
I can't do it alone." But while I'm listening
and sneaking a look around at the mess
and she repeats herself
there's a surprise:
Jeremy's hand is in my hand, he reached up for my fingers
at the same time she says, "I can't do it alone"
for her third time.

I say I'd like the job, but I have to ask my Mom.

"You have to ask your mom?" says Jolly,
and I tell her Yes I do. This Jolly with her 2 babies
looks at me and her eyes experiment with the word mom.

This is like a dare
and I tell her Yes again.

She's looking at me over the baby's head
and I say, "But I'll tell you tonight. I'll call you."
Jilly starts screaming
and we try to talk above the noise about when I'll call
and Jeremy is at my red shoelace again
and Jolly lets me out the door with its 3 locks
and I still hear Jilly screaming
all the way down the dim hall.

I might not be beefy to look at,
and on the home ec diagram back in 7th grade
my hair come out what they called
"drab, needs body."
But like they say appearance isn't everything.

4.

*T*his word COLLEGE is in my house,
and you have to walk around it in the rooms
like furniture.

Here's the actual conversation
way back when I'm in 5th grade
and my Mom didn't even have her gray hairs yet.
I'm sitting on the high stool in the kitchen
cutting up carrots and celery. You have to understand
this vegetable work would be a big deal for a little kid
which I was one then.
My Mom was putting the other stew things
together in the pot
and I was thinking about the movie they showed in school.

It was about how you go to college
and the whole place is all clean with grass planted
and they have lion statues and flowers growing.
You study in books and do science in a lab with microscopes
and you get to live in the dormitory and make popcorn.
Then you graduate
and you wear a cap and gown and it's outdoors.
Then you get a good job and you live in a nice place
with no gangs writing all over the walls.

I just up and asked her while we were doing the stew.
"Can I go to college when I'm big?"

My Mom turns her whole body to look at me
and she stops with the stewpot
and after she looks for a while she says,
"Nobody in this building"—
she waves her arm out sideways with the wooden spoon—
"ever went to college, nobody in my family,"
and she's pulling her chin up
and her shoulders and her chest, and she says,
no breath in between,
"somebody got to be the first, right?" And she goes back
to the stew.

Nobody in the building? It has 64 apartments.
I used to count the buzzers while I waited
for the squeaky elevator.
In 64 apartments nobody ever went to college.

She told me very clear, so I never forgot it yet
in all these 4 years since,
"You don't get college easy.
College takes 2 things,
money and hard work. And I don't know what else.
I never got there to find out.
Mostly you don't quit what you start.
You stick to the work you begin. You hear me, LaVaughn?"

I tell her Yes I hear her.
"We don't have college money, LaVaughn. You hear me?"
"Yes."
"You have to earn it. You listening to me?"
"Yes." This was brand-new news to me in fifth grade.

And some other time, maybe that night,
maybe another night,
she was saying good night
and have you done your homework,
and she said, "You go to college, you make me prouder
than I been in my whole life.
That's the truth, LaVaughn. I tell you."

And another time, I don't know when,
she says to me, she's blow-drying her hair to go to work,
she yells, "Listen here, LaVaughn,
what I said about we don't have college money?
You remember?"
I come around the side and yell up in her face
over the blow-dryer,
"Yeah, I remember."
She goes, "Well, we'll have a little bit. A little bit of it.
You earn it mostly, I can put in a little bit."
She swings the blow-dryer away and turns it off.
In her normal voice she says, "You'll make me proud.
Now get going. You be on time to school."
I reminded her I was never late to school.
She says, "See you stay that way, LaVaughn."

And she made a new account in the bank.
It's real little, but it's there. She puts a little bit in it
when she gets her check from the office where she works.
That's why that word COLLEGE is in our house
all the time,
it's why I babysit,
it's why I do all the homework all the time,
it's what will get me out of here.

We don't talk about it every day
but it's there.

My Mom sunk her teeth into this one,
this college idea. Every time I look like I'm forgetting college
she reminds me some way.
My Mom has an attention span that goes on for years.

5.

On the bus going home from Jolly's
I'm preparing my attitude for my Mom.
The way Jolly looked at me, "You have to ask your mom?"
Like she got rid of hers a long time ago,
like you'd put away a sweater.
But also she looked like it was a dangerous word.
Like she was blaming it.

My Mom is big, a big Mom. I'm riding the bus home
practicing saying to her I want to do this babysitting job.
I'd be sitting on the stool she keeps in the kitchen for
conversation.

We have 3 conversations most days. 1 in the morning
before she goes to work and before I go to school.
1 while dinner is getting made.
1 while we eat dinner. This is sometimes
a continued conversation.
Then it's homework time and no interruptions
and my Mom does her Tenant Council work,
she's the captain of the whole thing.
She makes her phone calls to the committees,
she staples the flyers together for the meetings,
she writes her letters to the mayor,
and still after all this time she believes
she'll get a personal answer.
She checks up on the Watchdog committee,

the way they got their shifts scheduled
so nobody gets in no door in the building
to sell drugs or do their pimping.

You can't trust the city to keep the bad elements out,
so the Tenant Council does it. Been doing it
since I was little. They carry their posters sometimes
all the way to the City Council:
"Public Housing Doesn't Protect Private Citizens."
Then the City Council argues about the budget
and my Mom and the others come home
and have another meeting.

Every night there's file folders all over the table
and phone notes on the counters
and my Mom's too concentrated on the latest problem
for even any conversation
so I usually go to bed without any
except Good Night and Yes I did my homework.

She notices me, for sure.
She notices I'm brushing my teeth
and piling up my books for morning.
She notices. She just usually don't take her mind off
the Council.

So while I'm on the bus practicing this conversation,
I'm thinking of the reasons my Mom could say No,
and I'm listing reasons I want her to say Yes.
I won't tell her about Jolly's mess, the whole mess it is
over there.

14

I line up my reasons:
1. I'll need mostly my own money for college.
2. The hours are OK, I can do homework
when the kids are in bed.
3. I babysat before, in our building. I know how.
One lady told me,
"LaVaughn, you got a feel for little kids, good for you."
4 is that sideways look of Jolly's eyes
like a car will come out of nowhere & run her down
but she partly hid her eyes from me
by wiping that gooey baby
& swinging her hair around.
5 is that sound in Jolly's voice,
that "I can't" she says over again.
I won't tell my Mom 4 & 5.
It's too complicated. My Mom would have opinions.
I'll tell her Number 6: It's 7 stops on the #4 Bus. Easy.
I'll tell her Number 7, about Jeremy holding my hand
by his own decision.

I get off the bus & I walk the half-block
and the Watchdog lady patrolling the street
nods her head at me
and I go in & I check the mirror
so I don't get in the elevator with no strangers inside.

The Watchdog lady today is a tough one, she teaches
the self-defense class for girls only,
every girl in the building takes the class,
you have to be 12 to get in.
They have graduation & everything.
I did it 2 years ago.

The elevator makes its squeaks & creaks & jerks
& in about a eighth of a minute I'll be saying my speech
to my Mom.

6.

"You know I was looking for a job, remember?" I start in
from the conversation stool at the end of the kitchen.
My Mom is putting oranges in the refrigerator drawer
and she hands me the Hershey's cocoa
to put up in the cupboard.
This is for hot chocolate from scratch,
the only kind we ever have.
My Mom won't have instant,
she says instant don't feel like a home.

"How many pages you got tonight, LaVaughn?"
is my mother's answer. She means homework. I tell her 9.
"So, you want to hear the job I can have if I want it?
It's babysitting, 2 little kids, evenings,
so their mother can go to work.
They're Jeremy & Jilly. I'd be their regular, their main sitter.
I'd be in charge."
I see my Mom's face going around the gaps I've left
in telling her.
"It's 7 stops on the Number 4 bus, easy," I say.
"The kids are real cute," I say.
"It'll be my money for college, like you always say," I say.

My Mom lays out the hamburger on the counter
from the grocery bag
and points to it with one hand and signs me with the other
to come & wash my hands along with her

to make the patties to freeze.
I get out the wax paper
and I tear the squares for the patties.

We stick our hands under the water, she spritzes the soap
and we wash our hands and then we patty up the meat.
"They potty trained?" my Mom wants to know.
"One's a baby, that's Jilly.
I think the boy's in diapers too," I say.
She digs out a scoop of meat, pats it.
"That's a lot of changing, LaVaughn."
She shapes the meat, slaps it, lays it down.
"That and all the wiping and the feeding
and your social studies and your math and all too."
I slap a patty down on the wax paper. "I can do it," I say.
The way Jolly said "I can't" repeats in my mind.
I pick up a scoop of meat.
My Mom breathes in deep, breathes it all out,
slaps meat on the paper,
says in her way, "Was there other jobs up on the board?"
"Yes," I say, and I tell her the notices I saw. Housepainting,
nursing home aide, housecleaning, janitor's assistant.

"What's their mother do?" my Mom wants to know.
"She does factory work evenings," I say,
concentrating on the meat.
I don't say she's 17, I don't tell her mess or her eyes.
"This going on all school year?" she asks.
I tell her Yes, and the summer too, if I do the job right.
My Mom likes the long-time side of the job.

This Jeremy, the boy, he held my hand
when I wasn't looking," I tell her.
She smiles at me over the patties.
That's a good start, LaVaughn."
And I see myself marching up the steps of a college
able to go to classes and get a good job of some kind of skills
and never live where they have Watchdogs and self-defense
ever again in my whole long life.

So I say, "Is that Yes?"
And she says, "It's a big job, LaVaughn."
And I say, "I know it is. I'll do it good."
She turns all the way to me from the meat,
holding a patty out to her side.
LaVaughn, you let those grades slip down, you'll be sorry.
Not from me. From your life you'll be sorry."
This is getting to be Yes, I can tell.
She slaps the patty down on the wax paper.

Can I call her then? She has to know."
You can corner even a big Mom like mine sometimes
when you have to have an answer in a hurry.
She looks at me, knowing this cornering,
and she sighs and she slaps the meat
and she says, "On condition.
On condition you keep those grades up.
You hear?"
  I tell her of course I hear.

Go to the phone," my Mom says, and I wash my hands and
  do it.

7.

*T*hose kids, that Jeremy and that Jilly,
were sloppy and drippy
and they got their hands into things you'd refuse to touch
They acted their age so much they could
make you crazy.

Then why did I keep going back?

I heard somebody say Jolly didn't face reality.
Jolly she says, "You say that?
Reality is I got baby puke on my sweater & shoes
and they tell me they'll cut off the electricity
and my kids would have to take a bath in cold water.
And the rent ain't paid like usual.
Reality is my babies only got one thing in the whole world
and that's me and that's the reality.
You say I don't face reality? You say that?"

I don't know why I kept going back.

But once, one night,
Jeremy woke screaming in a bad dream
and when I held him close
he shut up for a minute
but then he started again.

8.

Myrtle and Annie thought they had better jobs.
They predicted.
"Those kids'll get sick."
"A dirty place like that."
"You won't get paid."

By the time I went to Jolly's 4 times
Myrtle and Annie saw me skipping lunch to finish my math
and they took up their position.
"LaVaughn, this won't be a good job.
You gonna be too tired to keep your grades," says Annie.
"You work with us, you do it and go home.
That Jolly don't sound like just a job," says Myrtle.

But by that time my mind was made up.
Something made it up for me. It was clenched
like you'd clench a fist. I didn't explain to Myrtle and Annie,
not with them letting me know they didn't want to hear
about those babies
and their mom that was too young to be one.

9.

I could still quit, even when I was getting started,
but the very first week I noticed
there was a place
just above the leaf
hanging over Jilly's head
when she sat in her high chair
under the almost-dead hanging plant
and I was feeding her the yecchho yellow squash
from the jar I was sposed to heat.

It's that place—
just above the leaf—
a spiderweb is spun
and it's got no fly or anything caught yet.
It's that thready place of air. When Jilly hollered really bad
and I thought I was gonna crack open with the sound of it
the web would move
just so you could hardly see it
but it moved.

I wonder what Jilly would do
if she knew she could shake a spider's whole style of life
just by her sad hollering.

10.

*H*ere's how it was at Jolly's house:
The plates are pasted together with noodles
and these rooms smell like last week's garbage
and there isn't a place I can put my book to study for school
except places where something else already is.

The mirror is smeared with toothpaste.
The kitchen floor has the creamed spinach I spilled
a month ago.
I pull up a corner of the living room curtain and smell it:
you'd die.
You can't imagine the things that live
down the plugged drain.
Stuck in the high-chair corners are margarine
and rotting banana goo
and I got a C-minus on the social studies test besides.

If I get out of here to college, I'll get a good job. Maybe
I'll go to business college like a poster they have at school.
I'll work in a office and wear those jackets like you see
and I'll have my own filing cabinet
and also a desk with a calendar on it,
where you put your appointments down in the squares,
and everybody will know
"Oh, that's LaVaughn's department,"
and I'll never see a place like this again.

I look at my eyes in the mirror,
I put one finger up to wipe off
just a little bit of yuck off the glass
to see me better
and I'm afraid.

11.

I brought the pot and the dirt and the lemon seeds from my
    house.
Jeremy didn't know what I meant "Wait a while."
He didn't know
the lemon blossoms wouldn't come by Thursday.
I explained.
If you want something to grow
and be so beautiful you could have a nice day just from
looking at it,
you have to wait.
Meanwhile you keep watering it
and it has to have sunshine
and also
you talk to it.

So Jeremy goes, "Hey, lemon blom." And then he says,
"Go for it." And he sits right down in front of the pot of dirt
and watches.

I'm coming through with Jilly on my hip
and she smells bad like always
and her hands are full of sticky I don't know what
and I see
just an outline
against the sooty window
this little kid sitting beside an empty pot of dirt
and I guess he's concentrating or praying.

12.

*I*n social studies I got a whole country wrong.
On the map I forgot and I put
Angola where Zimbabwe is,
and then there wasn't any room for Zimbabwe.
They're in a whole far continent
and I missed them right in the U.S. 9th grade.

Here in this house it's the continent of, What do you call it?
What could you call it?
These kids never saw an ocean, so how could you explain?
You know what they see when they wake up in the morning?
They see the cockroaches climbing.
Even the roaches get driven up a wall here.
You could name them if you want. There are whole families.

And the drain is still plugged, the smell is deadly.
What can I say?

Zimbabwe took away some points
and I'll mess up something else and lose some more points
and my Mom will find out
and I'll have to quit Jolly
and I'll end up old and no college
with back rent to pay
and looking at cockroaches for my entertainment.

13.

Jolly came home. Two days she was gone
but she came home. I was sposed to leave before midnight
but there was nobody here
so I stayed.
Then there was nobody here still
so I stayed some more, the whole night.

A whole day of school I missed and my teachers
will turn their shoulders hard to the chalkboard
and say, Life is tough, here's your assignments due.

My Mom was in her outrage when I called late
saying I had to stay over. "Never again," she says
in her voice that at the same time pities the kids too.

Jolly didn't know she'd be gone so long.
She didn't even call.
She should call while she still has a phone.
She keeps not paying the bill, she won't have one.
But she paid me. Jilly held tight, pulling my hair
around her face, and her fists were like wrenches
fastened on.
I unclenched her and she was screaming
but I don't think Jeremy even noticed I was leaving,
he was at the lemon pot.

Jolly didn't look so good.
I didn't ask. I was curious
but I didn't want to know.

I know I won't end up like Jolly.
But maybe she thought she knew that too.

How do I study what I missed
when nobody was listening to tell me what I missed?
The social studies teacher says I could stay after
but I have to go to Jolly's then. The teacher looks at me.
I can almost see a movie going on in her mind.
I can't see how it comes out, who lives and who dies,
when she hands me a paper with page numbers on it.
I think I feel her hand in the air
almost reaching for my shoulder
but I turn fast and go away
with the page numbers in my hand.

14.

*T*here were only 3 diapers left so I said,
"Jeremy, you have to learn to go in the potty
like a man. You're a big boy now.
Jilly needs the diapers, you don't. Here's what you do."

I didn't know how to train him.
Why don't they show it on TV so he could imitate?
They show everything else he could do with his thing.

I lifted up the lid
and I pulled down his pants
and I said, "Now, go."
He didn't.
I turned on the water, it seemed like a good idea.
He didn't catch on, he walked away. I followed him
and pulled up his pants.

Only 2 more diapers left
and Jeremy wet his pants. I picked him up
and we went to the sink.
I washed him
and I washed his pants
and I washed the rug
and I washed my hands
and I didn't holler at him but I wanted to.

I told Jolly about the diapers.
She got some more.
I had tests to study for school,
I couldn't worry about Jeremy.

Guess what, I got A-minuses on 2 out of 3 tests
and I did it by studying. I was the only one in my row
to get Dakar. And then there's still
the potty at Jolly's, and I'm determined.
You should see me be determined. I go,
"Jeremy, this is a potty. That's your thing.
You're gonna stand right here at the potty—
right HERE—and you're gonna push till you go."
Jeremy looks at the potty
and he looks at my face
and his brain takes a hike somewhere
and so does he,
and I follow him and pull up his pants again
and I don't holler at him.

I get a warning slip in math
and I don't go to Jolly's for 2 days.
I see the stack of diapers is way down again.
Jolly likes Jeremy in diapers, I guess.
Jeremy's saying to the lemon pot,
"This is a pot, and you stand right HEOH
and you gonna GO." He truly shakes his finger at it.
I hold Jilly tight to my chest and I don't let Jeremy see
me laughing, I think I'm gonna explode with it.

Jilly crawls
behind the toilet

so I put her in the bathtub with her toys.
I hold her and sing about the whale coming up her leg
and I'm scrubbing smears off her face
when I hear the toilet lid go slamming down behind me.

I turn quick and I see just Jeremy's bare bottom
taking a hike out the door, dragging his pants on his feet.
I can't leave Jilly in the bath alone
so I quick grab her up in a towel and we check out the toilet.
Sure enough, it's yellow like it should be,
and we go running out of the bathroom, Jilly and me—
we're a committee of congratulations
and we don't slow down till we get to the kitchen
and Jeremy has his hand in the peanut butter
and his pants still down.

We look at him. "Jeremy," I say all serious,
"you pull those pants up now, you're a big boy."
He looks at me and Jilly
and puts a handful of peanut butter in his mouth.
I'm hoisting Jilly onto my hip
and tucking in the towel under her butt
and I'm reaching down to pull up Jeremy's pants
and Jilly's leaning over my shoulder
like a backpack with a face
and I can look Jeremy straight in the eye sideways
from down here
and I say, "You did it in the potty, didn't you, Jeremy?"
I want him to admit it.
He stares at me and at Jilly trailing down me.
"Congratulations, you're a big boy now," I say.

We look at each other and there's some monster secret
we both know
and he's smart enough to take it all solemn like it should be
and he pushes my hand away
and pulls his pants up all by himself.
They're crooked, of course.
They stay that way for a whole hour till he figures it out.

15.

Jolly came home bleeding and she
doesn't have folks.
"Nobody doesn't have folks," I said.
"I'm Nobody, then," she said,
" 'cause I don't." Her whole face was scraped
like it had a grater taken to it,
like it was cheese.

Jilly screamed when she saw it.
I was holding her when Jolly buzzed the door,
I couldn't hide her eyes
all of a sudden from her mother's bleeding face coming in.
Jeremy ran for a towel, he thought
a towel would cure it.
He's a little kid, how would he know
no towel's gonna cure a whole mess
of humankind?
It's the streets but I don't tell Jeremy this.

Jilly's screaming and Jolly's bleeding
and I'm asking where her folks' number is
and Jeremy's pushing a towel up her belly,
pleading she should put it on her face
and Jolly's standing all in the middle of us
with her eyes closed
and my vision is caught in an instant
by a cockroach going up the lamp, not in a particular hurry,

just going its time up the lamp, following a littler one
that's walked on ahead,
the lamp is glowing their shells all shiny
and they're moving up toward the light.
For just an instant I take time out, watching them.

Then I go back to the people in the room.
Jolly's taking Jilly from me, holding her against her neck,
and Jeremy's jumping out of the way of Jilly's kicking feet,
and he's wondering what to do with his towel,
and I look around and see I'm the only one not crying
in the whole house
so I go get the ice.

16.

Much as I hate to do it
I call my Mom
because Jolly doesn't got one.
Mom comes, bringing the first-aid kit.
"You don't got one of these,
where's your medical benefits,
you had your tetanus shot?
Somebody *shoved* you?" says my mother to Jolly.
She says the word "shoved" like attacking the room.

Jolly stood against the sink
with the ice on her face and watched my mother behave.
Jolly's eyes went undecided
and she leaned on her other leg for a while.
My mother made a clicking noise in her mouth and
used her thumbnail to dig some yuck
off a corner of the stove,
taking in the room with her memory.
I could see her listing dirty items.

"Well," she said, making her move,
"I'm your next of kin just for today. Just for today,
Miss Jolly. You need to take hold, girl. That's what you need."
She was telling her for her future.
"Now," my mother said,
moving in on Jolly who just watched,
"Gimme here that face, let's have a look,"

and in floating slow motion the ice came down
and Jolly's feet moved alongside my mother's
toward brighter light
and water started to run in the faucet
and I could see Jolly's cheek
floating on my mother's shoulder,
lying there all quiet
waiting to be healed.

My Mom lets me know what she thinks
later, at home, in the kitchen.
"LaVaughn, that Jolly's barely a child.
She don't have medical benefits,
she needs to take hold. She's a mess."

All at once I'm mad at my Mom saying this,
she don't know how hard Jolly tries.
But underneath I have to agree. I look at my Mom
to see if she's gonna take on Jolly,
the way she took on the Tenant Council. The way her face is,
it don't seem like she wants to.

And I remember how the sophomores look at the freshmen
like they're nothing.
And how the freshmen do to the eighth graders.
That's how my Mom is looking about Jolly.
It's looking down on somebody you're glad you're not.
"LaVaughn," she says, "if I knew she was so—
If you'd told me in the beginning—"
But then she goes soft, and she says,
"Well, you're a good help to her, aren't you, LaVaughn?"
I say Yes I am. I'm trying to be.

"Some people make a bad bed. They just have to lie in it."
It's this tone of voice of a mother
that comes out of her.
How could she be soft and sorry one second
and then be such a hard referee the next?

17.

"We're gonna tidy up around here,"
I say to Jeremy the very next time I sit.
"Dytie up?" Jeremy figures.
"Not exactly," I mutter, handing him a clean sponge
from the whole package of them my mother sent along.
"Squeeze it in the suds like this." I put his hand
and the sponge in the bucket of suds. "Now, scrub," I say,
and push his hand onto the kitchen floor.
Me, I go to the other corner
where it's worst.

Me and Jeremy get quiet and you'd think
this was the world's work,
like we're inventing a telescope
or building a Hilton hotel, we're concentrating so hard.
The sound of sponge and suds on the floor
makes us businesslike.
I show him the dipping and squeezing and he likes it.
I change the water, you don't want to know the color
and the things floating in it.
We use 6 buckets of hot suds and there's still our footprints
on the floor but you can see it's bluish now.

Our hands are pruny
and the smell has cleaned out our sinuses
and Jeremy stayed with it to the end.
I tell him he's a good boy. He says he knows it.

"Good boy sure," he says. I want to dig down way far
into his brain and find out some of his details.
How does he know? What makes him so convinced?
"Sure?" I say, still squatted on the floor,
wiping under the stove edge.
"Sure," he says, and holds his hand out to give me 5.
"5," he says. Little guy, he doesn't even know 3 and 4 yet.

18.

"*A*nd you're gonna learn how to make your bed," I tell
  Jeremy.
He's standing on it. "We'll pull the blanket up from here,"
I show him.
He squats and pulls and we make it mostly straight together
but there's a massive ridge of wrinkle underneath.
"We're gonna move that mountain," I tell him.
Back goes the blanket,
we smooth the underblanket and the sheet,
then the top again.
His hands are tough for pulling and lifting;
round little hands.

"You make your bed out of self-respect," I inform him.
He looks at me queer. "Bankets," he explains.

I don't say anything. I hand him his pillow from the floor,
spanking it with my hand first to dust it off.
"Where does this go?" I ask,
since he thinks he's so smart.
"Banket," he says. And puts it where it belongs,
with his head on it.
He lies down full flat on his back,
his feet sticking up orderly.

"Okay," I tell him. "You make your bed out of self-respect
and blankets." He has his hands folded, he's faking sleep.

With his eyes squinched tight,
he nods his head up and down,
lying flat as proud as he can be
of not understanding a single thing I've told him.

19.

*M*y Mom gets me at breakfast one day by her tone of voice.
"Verna LaVaughn," she says.
Even just when she says my whole name you can hear her
looking through me like a window
to those aunts that raised her.
She couldn't decide which one to name me after.
So I got both names.

"Verna LaVaughn," she says to me this time.
"That Jolly she's got hold of you."
I look at my Mom.
"You being around her all the time,
that's not a good example. You know what I mean,
Verna LaVaughn?
There's other jobs. You could look."

Now in my mind it's like trying
to find the right socks in a drawer.
You should always finish what you start.
You should help the ones that need you.
You should earn money and save it for college.
You should cherish your priorities like they say.
I'm hunting up there in my mind for the right thing,
and what comes up is this:

Jolly's TV set has got no vertical hold
and one night we turned the sound off and did our own.

Everything was rolling up the TV screen
and we said their words for them in different voices.
Jolly was the man with the weather map
and she reported with a bass voice,
"The whole world is rollin' up into the sky
with high winds from the northeast
and there is increased speeds of everything
disappeared into space."
And I got on sports and reported,
"Everybody hit home runs today,
all the balls went up, none came down,
and be sure you buy this brand-new car,
no money down, don't pay nothing till—
till—"
And Jolly she finished it for me,
"Don't pay nothing till you want to,
we'll just keep adding a kazillion percent interest,
oh, there goes the new car,
oh, there goes my toupee,
up into the sky. . . ."

And we laughed like fools.
Jeremy and Jilly didn't wake up.
Little spinning spongies flew out of the sofa
and the whole world was helpless,
rolling up colorful into the sky,
out of control
like tossing silk, like steady flame, like a joke.

This is definitely not what I tell my Mom.
"You maybe got a point there," I tell her,
to make her ease up on me. "I'll be careful."

"That's my girl," my Mom says. "You got college to go to."
"I know. That's why I sit the kids," I say,
and eat my eggs with pepper.

That was so funny, that night we did the TV voices.
Maybe it was only a couple of minutes. But.
You ever laughed so hard
nobody in the world could hurt you for a minute,
no matter what they tried to do to you?

20.

*S*o I'm imagining Jolly not having folks,
and how it must be not having any, not even one.
I'm doing my math on my bed
and it gets so frustelating as we say in our math class
I throw my pencil down and put my head back
and stare nowhere.
Up there on the ceiling the crack in the plaster
has a torn-paper shape
so there could be complete different worlds
on both sides of it
and then it branches like a tree hanging,
clear over to the window.

Sometimes I don't know if I remember the real day
or if it's just the photograph I know by heart.
In the picture there's my father and my Mom and me
and the bag full of picnic food
by the fence of a playground.
I'm standing between them
the way little kids do, all squirmy,
and I'm laughing up at my father
who must be saying something funny
just before the camera clicked
and my Mom is laughing too.
If you think I look young in that picture
with just my little sunsuit on and my little sneakers
just think of how many years ago that was for my Mom,

actually wearing shorts and laughing in the sunshine
like there's no problem.
Down at the bottom of the picture
you can just barely see my left hand,
it's so little inside my father's big right one,
and he is halfway through saying a word,
the way his mouth looks, like he never finished the sentence.

My father was a handsome man
and I almost think I remember that picnic. But maybe
it's just the picture.

My Dad he comes in little tiny pieces into my mind,
like those remnants, those samples you see
in the home ec room
where there's not the whole cloth. I get a glimpse
sometimes. Oh, of a part of his face, maybe, or hand.
Sometimes it's just a smell on the corner of a street
and then I quick look up and all around to find it
and it's gone around some corner
but there was my Dad
for just a walking step
passing by me
in a smell of back then
and he's gone. Sometimes I actually follow it—
even going down a street I don't need to go down,
but it never turns out.

21.

"*T*here was a little girl,
She had a little curl," I'm singing to Jilly.
Because you won't believe the things a baby can do.
Once they crawl, it's all over.
Wastebaskets, garbage, everything ends up
exactly where you'd put it last on your list of preferreds.
And herself.
How can you have so many coats of yuck on you?
Ketchup, hairs, coffee grounds, margarine,
like she's been painted by one of those painters.
And also she gets into Jeremy's things,
she dumps his barnyard puzzle
just when he's almost put it together
but looked away for a moment,
she topples his blocks,
she doesn't let him have the privacy of
his own ears, she's always reaching for them.

And she looks up, like Why Not?
Jilly isn't educated, that's all.

So, when she's good,
she pats Jeremy's hand in the stroller.
She lies sleeping in my arms like a pet would,
all pleated up in herself,
her eyelids completely patient,
her body would just fly if you threw it into the air

someplace on a starry night in the country
with grass around.
And her mouth goes open and shut for bananas so happy,
you could compose a whole song about
how a banana makes her more beautiful
than any daffodil blooming right in your face.
And she makes big eyes at the cockroaches,
like they're visitors.
When she's good she even likes such beasts as them.
And in the bath her bright fat gleams.

"Right in the middle of her forehead," I sing to her
and I touch it. It's her trademark curl, you might call it.
Her hair bends in such a way
to turn around twice in the front.
It even makes a shadow in the right light.
She smiles from my arms at the song
like I've just told her a hilarious joke.

"And when she was good,
she was very very good," I sing to her,
remembering her past and present good deeds,
mainly of friendliness.

And now Jeremy is paying close attention. He checks out
his own plain forehead.
He's listening close,
he wants to know how the song ends.
I work up a good memory of her messing around in things
you wouldn't go near in your right mind,
like sanitary napkins that aren't exactly brand-new.
And I sing with a strong voice,

"And when she was bad,
she was horrid." I make the last word very evident.

That part sobers her up
and she gives me her look. It's a studying look
and I know she's putting facts in her cupboard for later.

What I don't count on at that particular time is her brother.
It's later now, change of scene. I'm in a chair doing my math
and I honestly think they're both asleep.

And in comes Jeremy. "Looky," he says, holding up his hand
and from her bed has already come
a scream that the world is ending.
In Jeremy's hand like the Statue of Liberty
is a bunch of hair, clean sheared,
I quick look around his head—
How did he get scissors at his age,
what has he cut,
and where's the blood,
and will I be calling 911,
all these things I'm thinking at once.

But underneath I think I knew the instant I saw his face
the same time with her screaming. I absolutely think I knew.

I race down the hall to their room
and do I have to tell you what she looks like?
Jolly will have a quadruple fit, I know she will.

"Jeremy, I canNOT beLIEVE what you've DONE
to your SISter,"

my voice rings out as I swoop her into my arms
like I'm saving her from a revolution in the streets.

"Poor little THING," I'm wailing, top of my lungs,
"You could've KILLED her," my heart beating
into the side of her face,
and I look into his eyes real hard
and he sends me a telegram:

> If Miss Jilly don't have any more special curl
> she'll stop doing her bad things,
> I'm a hero
> and you don't even underSTAND.

And I bluntly learn something I'll never forget my whole life:
Stop and think before you whop a kid.
Every time, stop and think,
and count to a number you decide on.

I jounce Jilly up and down in my left arm
and I take Jeremy's hand with my right hand
on my way counting to 20,
and I look at the hair in his other hand
and we go to the kitchen
and I cut up an orange, their favorite,
and we all eat some.

22.

*S*o one day Jolly asks me about my Dad.
Where is he, do I have one.
Everybody asks sometime or another.

I don't want to tell Jolly everything I know
about how he died.
Your Dad dying is not something
you just have a conversation about,
it's a burden.
In this class I have at school, Steam Class,
they tell you how you can't be blamed for your burdens,
your burdens are things not your fault, you didn't do them
but you carry them around.
With my friend Annie it's 2 divorces,
and Myrtle it's too much drugs in the family.
With me it's my Dad died that terrible way.

I don't tell Jolly about the gangs
and how my Dad got in the way
on the blacktop that time
when him and his friends were playing basketball
and there was the shooting and my Dad was hit by a mistake.

What made my Mom so raging, as my Mom tells me:
He spent his whole life not being in a gang,
when he could be in one. In the neighborhood
that was the way.

But my Dad he went for sports and was on teams,
they got a trophy once from the city.
And then on a playground, underneath the basket,
the gang gun makes a lifetime mistake and hits my Dad
when it was sposedly aimed clear across into the alley.

I just tell Jolly he died when I was little,
and Jolly looks sorrowful for me.
"That's a sad thing," she tells me. I tell her I know it.
I was a real little kid. I even went to the funeral.
Sometimes my Mom says she don't know
if that was the right thing to do,
taking such a little twerp to the funeral
when my Dad was in a box they kept closed.
I tell my Mom it was better than having me not go
and always wondering where my Dad disappeared to.

I tell Jolly I went to the funeral and Jolly says
she went to one too.
I ask her how come,
since a funeral is not high on my list of things to go to.
She explains.
"It was one of my box guys—He did drugs and he died
and his folks showed up after he died
and gave him a send-off.
I went." Box guys? I ask Jolly.
"Box Guys and Box Girls. That was us. We lived in boxes
back of the Big Deal Hardware, where the overpass is."

Right away I ask Jolly did she really live in a box.
"Yeah. A fridge box. We all did."
She sees my eyes being surprised.

"People live in boxes, LaVaaaawwwwnnnn," she says.
"What do you think? Everybody has a house and a mom?
At first, your box is a little bit fun. It was summer, not bad.
We played cards, we found things in dumpsters.

"Later, it wasn't so fun.
It's like it ain't happening to you,
it's somebody else, you know?
It was the worst.
Nobody had folks. That Danny, the one with the funeral,
he had some,
but they didn't show up till he was overdosed & dead.
Then there was flowers all over the place—
the makeup on his face in the coffin made me laugh.
He looked like a doll."
I say out loud that's a bad thing to do to a dead person.
"But one thing for sure," Jolly says.
"You knew it was over.
You always knew where Danny was after that."
Then our conversation about death & dying was done.

I see how Jolly's burdens is probably too many to count.
Me, I got that big one, but at least I had a father.

The guy that shot the gun the wrong direction went to jail
for a while
but of course he got out. I hope I never see him
and on purpose I never found out his name.

23.

Jilly wouldn't go to sleep, she knew something.
Girls do, they sense things.
I'm walking with her, up and down the hall,
the roaches think we're on patrol
and they're hiding.

Something creepy was going on,
like lava moving so silent down one of those mountains
nobody knows how much there is of it.

With her being sleepless,
I put us both in the bathtub, mainly to change the subject.
Bathing with Jilly
is like going someplace warm into a tribe
and doing rituals. She decorates my face with suds
and fills the bathroom
with cooing sounds nobody but a baby makes,
like she's sending signals
to Martians.

And Jilly was right. There was something.
By the time Jolly limped in the door on her bad feelings
2 of us were clean.

Jolly comes in walking like somebody damaged,
you couldn't see blood but it was worse:
Fear.

You ever see somebody in great fear?
You know how they slant
like trying to hide from their own skin,
take another name, skip town on themselves?

Jeremy wants to show his mother his Silly Putty nose,
she puts him on her lap
but I don't know if she even knows he's there,
he's knocking his foot in the part of the sofa
where little cells of stuffing pop out and go into the air.

"I'm canned," Jolly says, and she translates immediately.
"Fired."
And I suddenly see, in piles,
all the food in the store nobody's gonna buy
for Jeremy and Jilly,
how Jilly has to be toilet trained right now
because of no more diapers,
not even soap to wash anything
and it's still so filthy around here,
and you have to have money to buy toilet paper, even.

I'm sick to my stomach thinking of the piles of things
but Jolly wants to explain
and I have to concentrate.

"My work it wasn't good enough, he said,
but it was like hers and hers so I didn't see the difference,
you couldn't tell looking at hers or mine who did what.
Same machines, same product, we all look the same,
I put my number on, every time,

they could check if they want."
Jolly's using her hands, thumbs out,
to show which hers she meant,
the her in front and the her behind
on the line. She's breathing hard.

Jeremy's looking up from her lap while she talks,
studying and blinking,
just staring up inside her mouth.

"Ain't my work," Jolly says,
and Jilly starts to cry in my arms. I jounce her.
Jolly and me look in each other's faces.
Jilly knows this one, too.
I just begin to wonder
along with Jeremy,
still staring at his mother's lips.

"Ain't my work," she repeats herself.
Jilly and me walk away and then back,
jouncing and howling.
Over the din of Jilly I watch Jolly's mouth go bitter,
I watch her hating something.
"So? What? Jolly? What is it? If it ain't your work? Jolly?"
I'm asking a stupid question, I find this out in a minute.
Jilly knows already somehow and she sets up a worse wail,
I want to whop her, stop her mouth,
and I change her to my other arm instead.

"Back of the office—
where they keep the—in a closet back there.
He touched me, way up under my shirt—

so fast I didn't even see his hand go—
he put his big old smelly wet mouth all over my face,
he was jabbin' my jeans,
I don't know how many hands he was usin',
maybe he got an extra." She looks at all of us.

"I said Stop it, he kept findin' other directions
to put himself all over me—
I put a pencil through his hand—
Made it bleed—
He said I'd be sorry—"
Jolly's mouth is poison with despising now,
you wouldn't want to go near her,
and she wants my opinion:
"Do I hafta wear a SIGN
says 'NO MORE MEN CLIMBIN' ALL OVER ME,
LOOK WHAT YOU DONE ALREADY'?"
And Jilly screams loud, that's her opinion,
and Jeremy he just stares up at his mother's moving face.
I push Jilly still screaming onto my hip.

Jolly's voice is real solid now, like car metal:
"I'll report him." And then her voice goes weak again.
And she goes more limp than she was.
Now Jeremy's holding her around her neck
and Jolly says, hard to hear,
"I need a job." She says, "You blow the whistle on them,
you're out of work for good."
"You ain't got a job now," I tell her.
"You been canned anyway, what you got to lose?"
This is a question she doesn't answer.

Jilly's just about out now, cried herself almost to sleep,
she hangs wet along me
tired from all that knowing,
her eyes closing and opening like silk curtains
with a pulse inside,
real smooth and real soft and
real slow.

"He's got a system support or what it's called,"
Jolly announces to me.
"So what's that sposed to mean?" I tell her, and she says,
"You got me, I don't know,
that's what the lady said in the bathroom,
he got a system support. Don't mess with him."

I don't like the glare of helpless hating in her face.
Jolly's almost four years older than me.
I tell her, "You were right the first time.
Yes, you can report him.
I'm putting Jilly to bed."
A book is laying beside her shoe on the floor,
I pick it up and almost slap it on her lap beside Jeremy's leg,
"And here, you read to Jeremy." It's one about a red truck.
"They never even think is it OK with you,"
Jolly says, weak-sounding.
"You mean bosses?" I ask her.
Jolly looks at me very hostile.
"Don't you know *any*thing?" she says.

Me and Jilly we walk out of the room,
and I change her and wash her and powder all her folds
and she's quiet, cooing at me, in and out of sleep,

and I tell her her folds are private, that part is hers,
it's precious
and she don't let nobody, not anybody,
ever go near her privacy
till she knows he loves her to stay with her her whole life.

What I don't know how is
how my killing anger at Mr. Fingers Boss
makes such tender love in my stomach for Jilly,
I could hold her close protected all night long
and not get tired.

24.

Jolly's fired, that means I've got no babysitting job
and I'm back where I started. My Mom gives me a look.

But Jolly's mad enough now, she's gonna do it.
I made her mad, her boss made her mad,
her fear makes her mad. It's her fear about not having a job.

The total number of times Jolly calls the factory
about her boss's behavior on the job
in the next three days is 11.
I know, because she gives me the daily report every night.
She phones me when she can get through
my Mom's Council calls.

"His other secretary answered, not the other one,
she won't let me talk to the boss of the boss,
he keeps being in meetings. She always says,
'And this is in reference toooooooo . . . ?'
and her voice goes up like that every time.
She pretends I didn't call any time before.

"He goes in his meetings,
he steps out of the office,
he goes in conference,
he goes to lunch. You can't get hold of this man."
I talk to my Mom on the subject of Jolly's situation.
Here's what she says: "That's sexual harassment,

Miss Jolly she'll need a lawyer."
"A lawyer?" I say. "She doesn't have Pepsi money
in her house."
"Anybody a witness?" she says.
"Me, only me, I saw Jolly when she came in her house."
"A witness to the incident."
"Incident," I say. "You mean him feeling her
and her putting her pencil in his flesh."
"That's right," says my Mom.

Jolly says of course there was no witness.
She says it like I'm stupid to ask, which I already knew.

Jolly makes the call 3 more times,
twice she gets secretary A, once she gets secretary B.
She calls me and says will I help her out
while she hunts a job.
I go there and I sit down with Jolly
and we make her list.
Jeremy wants to sit on my lap and then he doesn't.
He plays his pots & pans very loud
and he brings 4 books I should read to him
and I try to do it while we're making Jolly's list.

25.

*T*he list is really several lists.
Go to employment agency again.
Get Jilly her next shots that are due.
Get more roach exterminating powder.
Find out about a lawyer.
Get newspaper from neighbors and look in Help Wanted.
Add up exactly how much money left, total.
Find out how to get loan.
Count how much left in Food Stamps.
Jeremy's shoes get new ones.

And I find out a shock:
Jolly can't hardly spell her words.
I don't want to say anything about it.
She spells some of them OK.
But she doesn't know "neighbors," "exterminating," "exactly,"
and she spelled "loan" like "lone." Now this is pathetic
and her with two kids who can't spell either.
Who's gonna spell for her in her life?

So I get an idea, same time as she's getting one. We both say
we got an idea together. Hers looks urgent, so she goes first.
"How much money you got saved from sitting my kids?"

I feel my eyes narrow, like she betrayed me by thinking of it.
But maybe Jolly needs it more than I do?

That's my exit money. That money is in the bank
and it's getting interest right this exact minute
while she's asking me.
But I never been in such a bad mess like Jolly is.
I never had 2 kids and no job and the rent due.
But also I worked for that money.
I need it for some kind of college.
But she needs help right now.
I got more right to that money than she does.
But she's got more burdens than I do.

I feel my heart pumping vigorous.
I look at her and I say, "That won't help."
She thinks I mean there's not enough. I don't change my eyes
to help her misunderstanding. What I mean is
that money is not going to help her
because it's saved to help me
not end up like her.
I feel very mixed but my eyes stay steady.

Jeremy comes dragging the book
about the crab on the ocean floor
that grabs at anything it finds,
and Jolly says she can't read to him now,
and I say, "Then how's he gonna learn to read,
somebody don't read to him?"
Jolly looks down at the list we're making
and I take Jeremy beside me and we read the book
about the crab under all that water
trying to grab onto everything till in the end it grabs
the pirate treasure, a chest of gold.

26.

*T*hen is the time the word COLLEGE came more real again
since way back in 5th grade when I saw that movie
and told my Mom.
COLLEGE was then sposed to be my priority all the time.
But I used to forget.

Once I even looked at the bank book,
I was in 8th grade, and I figured I could do these things
with the money I already had there from babysitting
and returning bottles:
Get a perm, get 3 new sweaters, and buy ice skates
like the Olympics to go to the rink
with one of those little tiny skirts they wear.

I had the good judgment to not say anything to my Mom.
Annie and Myrtle were promising to take skating lessons
and we all 3 got filled up with our hopes to do so.
Every single one of us couldn't do it in reality,
even when Myrtle's mother promised to pay but she lied.

Then there was this time with Jolly.
Jolly thinking I could give her some of my money
or loan her some
which I knew immediately she couldn't pay back.
I went back and forth about it in my mind
but my eyes never said so.

What I knew at the end of the conversation
was this information:
I knew exactly where that money was aimed for.
Never no doubt at all.
My little kid brain got sidetracked once in a while.
But never no real doubt on the subject.
I was going to get out someday not very long in the future.
It would be college for Verna LaVaughn
and a good job and not any despair
like I saw in these surroundings here.

27.

*F*inally, Jolly gets around to asking me my idea.
Jeremy is in the bathroom
sitting on the edge of the basin washing his feet
and Jilly is in the playpen teething on a carrot
I thought of.
Jolly asks me how come I thought of the carrot.

"You want to know my idea," I said.
She nods her head.
"My idea is you go back to school.
When you last went to a class, Jolly?"

Her eyes go scared but she pretends it's tiredness.
"Me go back to school, you got another joke?" she says.
"No, I am completely serious," I tell her. I walk away,
I check out Jeremy in the sink
who is having a joke with his toes.
I come back and there's Jolly staring at the wall.
"I had a job, I earned good money," she's saying.
She's telling it to the lampshade.

I look at her regretful face
and I tell her what my Mom told me.
"The Welfare Reform," I tell Jolly.
"You gonna get Welfare for these—"

"Welfare!" she says, jumping off the sofa,
sending a spray of foam whirlies
behind her legs. "Welfare! Not in my life, never
no Welfare ever again!"
She bends down and gets Jilly into her arms,
now Jilly's covering her whole front like armor,
"We don't want no Welfare!" she says like it's a disease.
"Do we, Jilly?"
And Jilly and Jolly stare at me with related eyes,
mad and scared.

I try to picture Jilly's father, what kind of guy he might be.
He said Jolly had a real cute nose, she told me once.
She never told me what Jeremy's father said. But they had
something in common: They both left babies when they left.

"My Mom told me about it," I go against her look.
"She says you register at school, you go for your G.E.D.,
you and them get—"
Now Jolly has managed to clench Jilly in between her arms
and get her hands over her own ears at the same time,
she won't listen to me
in spite. "Don't say to me your Big Mama said!"
Jolly yells at me.
This name takes me by surprise.

I go get Jeremy down out of the sink.
He tells me about the crab
that ate his toes all up in the water and I say that's too bad
because we were just gonna have a snack
of toes and orange juice,
too bad for us. Jeremy slaps me 5.

"You know what they do, Welfare gets hold of you?"
Jolly is telling me.
"They take your babies, the state takes your *ba*bies—
I seen it happen—They find out you got no job,"
her voice is raising,
"no fathers for your babies,
they see you live in a poor house, they say you—
AIN'T A ADEQUATE PARENT."
She huffs & looks at me for my answer.
I don't say any. I don't have any.
Jolly says she saw it happen, I believe her.

"They make you a charity case,
then they take your babies," Jolly is going on,
keeping Jilly up close to her.

I got math homework to do so I tell Jolly I'm leaving.
"You don't need me," I tell her,
meaning she won't listen anyway.
And I walk out the door which you have to close twice
or the first lock of all three locks won't lock.

Now there is a pile of things between me and Jolly.
One is money, she can't pay,
and do I stay with the kids out of love?
Two is "Welfare!" the way she hollered, she won't listen.
She already saw the state take babies away.
Three is I go to school and I'll be out of here.
Four is money too, she don't know how much I saved,
I didn't tell her.
Five is Jolly doesn't want to hear of my Mom
because my Mom said "You need to take hold."

She called her my Big Mama.
Six is I think of a carrot to teethe on
and Jolly can't think of that.
Seven is Jolly can't spell her words.

part two

28.

I'm going back to Jolly's after school while she hunts
   a job.
She can't pay me but she will when she gets one.
This is something I don't discuss much with my Mom
because of the sound she makes in her mouth
clicking air when the subject comes up.

I get up my nerve
on the 4th day Jolly comes back with no work,
and I ask her: "How did you get hurt that time,
that time with your face?"
It's healed by now, but her hand goes up to it
and she tells me it was just somebody she saw that day,
"Just one of the kids I used to hang with.
He got mad I wouldn't tell him where I live.
He got all up in my face,
all 'Baby I want to do you good,'
all 'Jake & Indian Ken & Angel miss you,'
all that talk. I told him I got a life now,
I don't want no dealings with any of them,
he got mad I wouldn't tell him my address.

"I shouldn't go back there. I ain't going back.
Even the neighborhood,"
Jolly says, and I see Jolly is a magnet for bad luck.
I wonder did she ever know anybody nice.

"But I don't got a life now, do I, LaVaughn?" she asks me,
and I don't want to agree with her
but she's got no job, so what can I say?

29.

One time I had to answer my Mom about Jolly's situation, being that my Mom asked. She knew I wasn't getting paid for these times of sitting. It was early in the morning before school. She commented on me going to Jolly's again that day.

I worked on explaining. "Jolly she's gonna get on her feet. She's had bad luck. I don't know, it's like—"
I'm putting on my sweater and putting my math book in the backpack.
"It's like, you know how a bowling ball goes, when somebody bowled it crooked? It goes into the what do you call that place?
You know, when it goes sideways . . ."

My Mom is giving a last swoosh with the sponge to the counter.
She says, "The gutter is what you call it, LaVaughn."

I leave for school not forgiving my Mom for saying that.

30.

*J*eremy is still mad at the lemon seeds
for not being a lemon plant. He thinks it's a lie.
I'm taking him to buy shoes
and while I'm squatting down to tie his old ones
that are too little,
I understand how he sees
everybody's knees. And the bumpers of cars.
And under tables. That's his line of vision.

If you're that short,
and you've learned to go in the toilet
and not to hit your baby sister all the time
and besides that your mother got fired
and she's going around yelling,
and somebody's told you there'd be a lemon plant
and all you see is wrinkly, stickery dirt,
no wonder you'd be mad.

I'm tying his too-small shoe with the knotted lace,
and I can't just keep on coming back without pay,
and Jeremy wants a nice life like everybody else wants one,
and he has his hand on my shoulder as I'm squatting down,
and I look straight across into his eyes
and I wish all of a sudden most in the world, more than
I wish somebody should fall in love with me, even,
I wish I could do magic to make the lemon plant grow.

It's when we're going to the shoe store I find out
about Jeremy and buses.
"There's our bus," I said, when I saw it coming
like a flat-faced animal along the street.
"Shoe bus?" says Jeremy.
"Yeah," I say, "there's our shoe bus."
Jeremy stands up straight,
his striped shirt sticking out in the sunshine,
and he's gonna be sure he boards that bus right.

In our luck we get the kind of driver says "Good Morning,"
and Jeremy says up to him, "Get shoes."
"Yes, sir," says the driver back down at him
and we find ourselves a seat.
Jeremy sits tall and rigid, trying on bus-sitting.
He goes alert at the bell ringing,
and I tell him he can pull the string when it's our turn.
I hoist him on my lap to watch what's going by.
He concentrates out the window and studies
the man spitting on the sidewalk,
the old lady with spidery arms
lifting her walker two inches at a time,
two boys chasing a cat.

This is better than a movie, I decide,
and since Jolly's TV has got no vertical hold
I might as well bring Jeremy on the bus for his excitement.
He shows me out the window a big dog
and makes a growl,
he puts all his fingers flat on the glass and his nose too,
pressed still.

Then what he does, he puts my purse on his head,
it's his crown and I quick understand:
He's King of the Bus,
King of the Shoe Bus,
we're all his surrounders, his servants.
The driver is driving us to the shoe store
because we ordered him to,
back there when I said "There's our bus."
Jeremy found out, and he's in charge.

I look at Jeremy's king face,
I tell him he can stand up and pull the string now,
he gives me back his crown to hold while he does his job,
I hoist him to the string,
he makes the bell ring,
we prepare to unload ourselves,
and he announces to the driver when we leave,
"Get shoes."
"Yes, sir," says the driver,
and the bus makes the air-hissing sound,
and we're back down on earth
to buy shoes
we can't afford.

31.

*A*t the shoe store they don't think we're serious customers
so they ignore us.
We're out for an amble on their thick carpet.
But Jeremy starts his dance.
He saw a man playing Hacky sack last week,
and he goes into his Hacky sack dance
whenever he remembers.
His legs go out like umbrella pieces and it's hilarious.
A clerk with a rash on his hands comes up & says,
"You, gal, get that little boy."
I don't tell him this is an unfriendly way to sell
his expensive shoes to people.
I don't tell him not to give me orders.

I look at the shoe prices
and I think how Jeremy grows too fast
for his mother's money. I've memorized Jeremy's things.
He has boots for rain puddles, he has socks,
but too-tight shoes.
I see some on a rack, they're blue and white, nice shoes,
and I ask Jeremy
how about them. He sings, "Get shoes, Hacky kass,
Get shoes, Hacky kass,"
and the way it ends up is this:

Jeremy's shoes cost what Jolly would pay me
for 6 hours of sitting.

79

I look at Jeremy wearing his new, good-fitting shoes,
doing his dance,
and I put the money up on the counter, and I know it's okay.
I figure I don't even feel bad about it. Matter of fact,
shopping for shoes with Mr. Jeremy is fun.
I don't need to get paid
for having fun. And that's the way I feel.
And that's that.

32.

I'm riding home on the #4 bus after Jolly's one night
when I catch one of those waves of my father, it just goes by
in an instant. I look back & I don't even know what it was.
A store going past the window,
or somebody's sleeve on the bus.
I never see it fast enough.
But then my Mom comes into my mind
& I think how it was back then,
with all the vagueness of my remembering.

What my Mom did is like a foggy photograph,
like one you might think you dreamed.
I don't even remember her at first.
At first when it happened.
Then I remember her huge.
She got huge. Like she multiplied.
I never figured it out, but she was big.

I don't mean fat. She's average, you could say.
It's a bigness about her she got some way,
not a bigness she could diet off.

I remember thinking, in first grade,
the other kids had little moms.
Their little voices, their little hands.
Even little shoes, I think they had.

I got used to having a big Mom,
that was the way it was. Still is.

And another thing:
You know in September
when your mom gets you the pack of 3-ring paper
to go in your binder?
How much does she get for you?
You know how much my Mom buys?
It's this stack that's so high, like a phone book.
In 4th grade I used it as a weight on top of the flowers
I was pressing for presents. The ones from in the park.
Mostly yellow ones, buttercups,
but forget-me-nots too. Those are blue.
I kept them under the big stack of 3-ring paper
till almost Christmas
when it was time to make presents.
And my Mom thought I was going to do that much math
and spelling.

And when I gave her those buttercups and forget-me-nots,
all pressed into a picture,
she held the present in her big hands
and she said in her big voice,
"I'm proud.
LaVaughn, I'm proud you can make a flower picture
so good, all blue and yellow like that."
And I had just a glance of a father, somebody's father,
liking the flower picture too. Just a glance.
And she looked at my hands and she said,
"Those hands did good work, didn't they, LaVaughn?"
It wasn't even a question. But just that glance

of my father liking the picture—
I don't know how it came into the room.
But it came there.
And I think it must be her big voice and her big hands.

33.

*M*e and Jeremy are saving other seeds now
to grow a garden. I brought 2 more pots from home
and dirt besides. So Jeremy's eating oranges real fast,
and a peach. And we go shopping with the Food Stamps
that are left.

Jeremy sits on the underside of the shopping cart,
the bottom rack
where you would put huge things
like a great big bag of dog food.
He's happy under there, he's a lion at the zoo,
as he tells me in front of the canned beet shelves.
He says my name:
"Bon see lion zoo?" He holds on to the cart like it's his cage,
scoping out the legs going past.

Now I start to pretend to be down there,
I begin looking just at legs and feet parading
past the magazines on the rack
about how a lady gave birth to a Martian
and the father of the baby is suing for visiting rights.
Down there is where bubble gum and lost shopping lists go,
stuck to the floor with bootprints on top,
and celery pieces and used pacifiers and spilled coffee beans
from the gourmet grinder.

I look down there
and that's where you see the toes of people
and their hairy ankles
and their untied shoes
and the feet of the dry shrunken ladies
when their sons take them shopping.
Up higher you hear their voices
making some last request,
you see their sons go along with it,
some kind of creamed corn or oxtail soup in a can,
and you see their sons stop trying to talk them out of it.
But way down below
where Jeremy is
you just hear the scraping of their shoes
across the spilled rigatoni pieces,
and the limping old legs,
these old ones that haven't given up yet.

I'm thinking that's why they want kids to ride up top
of the cart cruising the grocery store,
up there where the world
isn't such a dying, garbagey place of discards.
I'm about to invite Jeremy up top
and I bend down to get the Pepsi 6-pack and I hear
near my knees,
Jeremy's sending a message real soft,
sending it to the knees of strangers:

    Balloon Balloon Balloon Balloon

    Balloon Balloon Balloon Balloon

    Balloon Balloon Balloon Balloon

    Balloon Balloon Balloon Balloon

                Balloon

34.

I took Jolly with me to my Steam Class.
First we arranged the kids.
I kept telling her and telling her
they have Day Care there but she had excuses.
"They'll get sick from the other kids.
Jilly'll holler.
Jeremy'll forget and wet himself."
Of course she really was afraid to go.
Three years ago
she left school for Jeremy and was gonna go back
and was gonna go back
till she had Jilly
and there was no more gonna left in her.

So we got them ready and the giant bag of kid stuff, too,
and we got on the bus. Now Jeremy thinks a bus ride is
next to heaven
and Jilly finds a lady behind us to babble to
and we make our bus ride with no accidents.
Then Jolly sees the great big carved words
HIGH SCHOOL and she goes
into her shame style which she makes look like
stuck-up snobbery.
She walks different, her whole body shifts its gears,
she goes into Underdrive, you might call it.
Jeremy looks up at her, checking out her uneasy eyes,
and he returns to staring at our surroundings.

Jeremy never walks, always dances,
there's a band inside him giving him rhythm,
and he's dancing among the school kids
and all of a sudden I see they're dancing too.
They shimmy and wiggle and lurch in all their colors,
and if I squint my eyes it's a circus,
somebody ought to sell cotton candy,
and there should be confetti.

So in we go to Day Care and I point out
who Jolly and Jilly and Jeremy are.
I say we'll be back after the next period.
I see Annie's sister in there,
working, who explains she's an apprentice in Day Care now.
Jolly looks around
and sees 2 adults and 2 apprentices and 4 babies
and she's amazed it's so simple.
I explain to her: "I told you, this is what they do.
This is what they *do*."
Jolly can't get over how it's so easy,
and I make sure she notices how clean, too.
Jeremy instantly goes for the blocks,
he's gonna have himself a build,
and by the time we leave, a lady is singing Jilly a song,
stopping her hollering.

Jolly's in Underdrive all down the hallways,
only she puts a shimmy with it, too,
so she's sending such signals
to the onlookers she imagines are looking on,
she's walking in double language.
We go in the door to Steam Class

and I say I've got a visitor and they say OK,
and Jolly goes mute.
We sit in the circle like always.

I'll explain: They began it called Self-Esteem Class
but everybody resisted.
The story goes that one day the teacher said,
to the few kids who came in anyway,
"Okay, everybody, now you go out of here
with your assignment to BE YOURSELF
and you work up a good head of steam,
and you do it enough times
and nobody'll knock you around.
You ever hear of anybody a*bus*ing a steam engine?"

And now it's called Steam Class.
They changed it on the computer and everything.
And they're turning people away on waiting lists.
We go in & Jolly gets silent.

"The word for this week, as you all of you know, is
CAPABLE," says the teacher who's long and tall
and wears nests of rings
and has let her hair get gray in places and today
has a purple dress and running shoes on.
"We'll go around the circle and you say,
'I'm capable of,' and you finish the sentence
how you want to. Go."
The circle starts. Eleven people are in Steam Class today, and
everybody has to say something. Whoever makes a joke of it
can get an F in Steam Class for not being serious.

DON'T DEMEAN is written on a big poster on the wall.
Jolly doesn't get it
because nobody's explained her the word yet.

"I'm capable of passing my driving test."
"I'm capable of not hitting my sister."
"I'm capable of, I'm capable of, of, of, of,
I'm capable of, of, I'm capable of, of finding my MATH book."
This is Jamie, he takes his time.
"I'm capable of staying sober today."
"I'm capable of graduating high school."
"I'm capable of my accounting homework."
"I'm capable of I won't let Him hit me."
This is a Him we hear about every class,
and we keep telling her to
get rid of Him. She doesn't want to yet,
He has some kind of hold.

They go around the circle saying their capables
and Jolly is going stiff on her chair.
She has her "This is stupid" look on.
I see the teacher eye her fast
and move on. I lean to my left just enough
to let my shoulder touch Jolly's shoulder,
I'm passing confidence through the clothes and muscles
but her shoulder doesn't feel like it gets it.
Maybe she conducts it
right through her to the next person
like electricity.

My turn was coming before her. I knew a whole set of things
but I decided on one about Jolly's home life

and I said, "I'm capable of giving Jilly a good bath.
That's Jolly's baby here," and I point my head to Jolly.
Now it's Jolly's turn and she goes completely limp.
I poke her. The teacher sees whatever it is in Jolly's eyes
and says, "It's okay, you're a guest this time.
Guests don't have to
if they don't want to."
If Jolly was to tell you about that moment
she'd say "I was invisible. I wasn't there."
But I'm a witness and I know she was.
I saw three sets of eyes in the circle get superior
and I saw the teacher raise her hand like smoothing her hair
but her thumb was in a subtle way pointing to the sign
she got disgusted enough to make last week on the wall:

> COMMON DECENCY IN THIS ROOM AT ALL TIMES.
> AND DON'T YOU EVEN *DARE* PRETEND YOU DON'T
> KNOW WHAT THAT IS.

So Jolly got incomplete benefits from the class that day,
but she lived through it. You don't learn your Steam
till you have to talk
and keep talking.
It takes some people longer than others.

And I went home without any pay
of course.
Where's Jolly gonna get any money to pay me?
But I stood in the shower, shampooing my hair
from the peanut butter Jilly dragged through it,
and I laughed and laughed. What was so funny, you ask, was
how me and Jolly and Jilly and Jeremy must have looked,
on the bus, and in the hallway,

and on the sidewalk where we had to stop
when Jilly's pacifier fell out of her mouth
and bounced on some dog poop.
We must have looked like some kind of family
going along in our separate kinds of walks:
Jeremy dancing his Hacky sack dance,
Jolly shimmying her shimmy of
"I got no problems, no babies' dads disappeared on me
and I ain't been fired from my job,"
Jilly bouncing on my arm and humming
and leaning out from my hip like a flag waving itself.
A family from the continent of I don't know what.

35.

We had fish at my house and I picked up the lemon seeds.
My Mom saw me washing them at the sink
and she asked.
I was taking them to Jeremy
since his didn't bloom. "That Jolly she's in some disrepair,"
says my Mom. "What you think she's gonna do?"

With my Mom sometimes it's like an exam,
she gives no respect to waiting around.
Her motto is
    Bootstraps go in 2 directions,
    either up or down.
    You choose
    and you remember you chose.
She learned it from her aunts.

Proof is, she says, we pay our rent exactly on time
and we have insurance benefits from her job
in case of catastrophe
and we go to the dentist
and in taking care of ourselves we don't mess around
waiting for somebody to do it.

This motto is on her face
while I'm running water on the lemon seeds.
"Some just can't gather themselves together," she says.
"When did you get paid last?" she says.

She already knows exactly.
"Why isn't that girl back in school?" she says.
"Why's she have TWO babies?" she says.
"Any cleaner around there
than when I saw, she was all cut up?" she says.

I pretend the water's running too loud to hear.
Nobody felt my Mom up in a closet
and then fired her,
I don't think. I turn around and look at her from the faucet.
No. I'm sure nobody did.

"You talk like it's her fault," I said, turning off the water
and I start.
"Don't start with me," she says. "I didn't say 'fault,'
I said 'gather together.' She needs to take hold."

"She needs time," I say.
"Rent won't wait," she says.
"Next thing she'll be wanting to borrow."
I don't tell my Mom Jolly already tried that.
We're looking at each other and I see her suspicion.
She says, "She wants Welfare, she can't get it,
they won't give it if she hasn't got her education.
What's she gonna do?"
I think about Jolly hollering "Welfare!"
and I don't know the answer.

"She's looking at jobs," I say.
"And you're sitting the kids free after school," she says,
accusing me of it.
I look at her and wonder if sitting them free

is more wrong than right,
more right than wrong,
and I take my handful of lemon seeds
to a paper towel and I lay them out, counting.
I don't know why I'm counting them.
What I know is
it's better they have me with them, not yelling
than Jolly who yells.

Four jobs turned her down,
and the one she got lasted four days
because they found a Band-Aid in the chowder
and blamed her.
She hasn't got references from Mr. Fingers Boss.
I'd yell, too.

My Mom shrugs her shoulders
the way they must have taught her in Mom School
before she came down to earth to get born a mother,
and I take my English and my math and the lemon seeds
and I go. Those aunts must have taught her that shrug.

I haven't closed the door yet when my Mom calls,
"How many pages you got?"
Number of pages of homework to do.
I tell her. 11.
"You be sure you don't do 10," she calls to me.
I hear her echo off the door panel: 10, 10, 10, 10, 10.
They train Moms to have that voice that echoes
or they don't get to be Moms.

36.

*B*ut Jolly wants Jeremy to think those are the originals he
   planted before.
"He should have *his* lemon seeds bloom," she says,
trying to make me agree.
"Sneak 'em into the dirt and he'll never know."
She turns her back.

I look at her. She's his mother, she should have the choice.
I imagine a picture of what happens:
      These seeds bloom and Jeremy doesn't know
      I sneaked 'em in.
      He's all proud of what he did with nature
      and what do I do but praise him too, lying.

"No, that's wrong," I tell Jolly. She turns right around
and wants me to prove it but same time is afraid to say so.
"See, Jolly," I say, and then I don't know what comes after.
My hands stand straight up at my sides
like those chicken wings you see,
all bent, that's probably why chickens can't fly.
"See, Jolly," she whines, imitating me,
doing her arms like mine
and we laugh.
We're covering the principle of the thing with a joke.

What happens is Jeremy by himself solves it.
Coming into the room he inquires.

"My seeds?" he says, over at the chair
I laid them on in their towel.
I see Jolly out of the corner of my eye
changing her mind about lying.
"New seeds for your lemon pot," she tells him.
"These ones are gonna grow," she promises,
like now Jolly runs nature
and decides which things will live and which will die.

Mr. Jeremy takes his new seeds and he gets a chair
and he climbs up to the pot
and he puts his fist of seeds over the dirt
and a brief light comes around him from the window
and he looks just like those picture books.
Where Mom wears an apron, Dad comes home from work,
cookies are always coming out of the oven
and everybody has those NO PROBLEM
looks on their faces,
the worst that could happen,
the cat might tip over the water dish.

For just a second, Jeremy looks like that. I'm surprised
and I take a picture of him in my mind for later.
Then everything goes back to the way it was,
you can smell Jilly's throwup,
there's sticky stuff on the floor,
the dishes are dirty because they ran out of soap,
flies are buzzing around Jilly's cup
and I go get Jeremy some water for his lemon tree.

37.

I get an idea and I ask Jolly. It takes courage to ask
because of the look in her eyes.
"Jolly, what about those fathers?" I say one night.
Maybe it was the smell from next door,
meatloaf or some family food.
Her eyes go slitty. "What about?" she imitates,
trying to sound dumb.

"I mean, don't they owe *some*thing?" I'm taking a chance
on her getting mad. She looks hard at me,
daring me to say more. "Look, Jolly," I go.
"You didn't have those babies, you'd finish school,
you'd have a job, you'd have—" I stop because
I pictured her in a prom dress and corsage, and
that's a thing you wouldn't want to say in front of her
when Jilly's slurping air, fast asleep on a blanket on the floor,
with her bare foot stuck out
like something she won't be needing.

Jolly looks down at me even though we're the same height.
"So?" she says, quite slow.
I think it's the way she puts her feet up across the sofa,
her total limp body lolling, and the way her hand
reaches for the nail file
and the spark of Night Danger Red nail polish
that shoots in the air
from her left middle finger and disappears

as she says, "I'm doin' okay. . . ."
that gets me going.

I look at her like I haven't done before. I feel a machine gun
in my head not going off, I feel lightbulbs turning up bright
in there, I feel a microphone against my brain.
"No, Jolly," I say.
I hear myself begin.
"No, you're not. You're not doing okay.
The kids need their vegetables,
you got maybe six squares of toilet paper left,
every time the rent comes due there's a panic—"
She's filing two fingernails at once, she's got a system.
I go ahead and continue.
"At least one of those dads, he ought to know.
Wouldn't he like to see—"

Slam goes the fingernail file,
pinging the edge of a Pepsi can,
Jolly upheaves herself off the sofa,
sponge stuffing poofs around her, she goes to turn on the TV,
she says, "Those guys both, they can go rot.
Let's watch TV."
Jilly turns over and sniffles up inside her nose
what was oozing out of it
and the man on TV says we can win a trip to Hawaii.

And I know nobody on TV is going to do my homework
and I don't want to do it either,
all those maps and semicolons
and binomials, but they're my ticket out of here,
so I pick up my books and get my stuff. Jolly knows

she owes me now for 19 hours of sitting
and I tell her See You Later
and she waves to me as I go out the door.

I'm mad going home.
There was that feeling of the machine gun
not going off, there were those bright hot lights inside,
there was me knowing something had to get done
and knowing Jolly wasn't going to do it and I'm mad.
I kick a candy wrapper under the seat in front of me
on the bus,
I listen to my teeth scraping each other,
I watch it begin to rain out the window,
and there's that microphone against my brain
and I don't know what to say into it.

38.

*N*ext morning I woke up and I remembered.
One of the people on my Mom's Council,
he used to be a boxer.
My Mom always says he always says Get up on the 1,
You don't want them to count 2,
'cause then it's easy to count 3
while you go on being down. Always
Get up on the 1.

I remembered it.
They could be counting 6, all the way down to 9
while Jolly filed her fingernails,
and me, I jumped out of bed.

"You're shot from a pistol this morning," said my mother.
"You did all your pages?"
I did them in bed, and I tell her so,
we give each other thumbs up
and she goes off to her job
and me to school.

I get my quiz back in math and I see I missed 3 in a row,
all the same kind,
and just in an instant I see what I did wrong.
The teacher makes you do them over so you learn.
I finish in nine minutes.

"You're shot from a gun this morning, aren't you?" she says
when I turn in my corrected quiz. "Yes, ma'am," I say.
"You got those all fixed?" she says.
"I sure did," I say.

I get to my Steam Class early,
and I go, "You remember my friend Jolly I brought here?"
The teacher today is in an orange sweater,
bright like melted ore in the science book,
and she's standing by the filing cabinet.
She looks at me. "Yes," she says.
"The one who doesn't have her capables."
"That's the one," I say.

I make myself the authority on Jolly and I say,
"She's in trouble."
The teacher makes the answer Of Course
with her eyes only. So what else is new? her eyes ask me.
I make the list:
Jolly has her two kids, no husbands, got fired,
but I don't go into the subject of getting up on the 1.
The teacher would be there too fast
having somebody make wall posters of referees' fingers
and bodies climbing up out of flat positions.

"She get Public Assistance?" The Steam teacher asks me.
No, I say. She won't give in.
"How's she paying for their shots
and well-baby doctor visits?"
I think back and I don't remember about the second part.
"What's a well-baby doctor visit?" I say.
It's then I start understanding what Jolly's leaving out.

You take a baby, even somebody big as Jeremy,
they're sposed to go to the doctor
for checkups. Their ears and eyes and things. Their throats.

What jobs she's been fired from,
the Steam teacher wants to know.
I tell her. She says, "Minimum wage, how does she expect?"
I tell her I don't know.

The Steam teacher steps back to take a look at me
up and down.
"You sit for this Jolly, right?
You're going on to further education
on the babysitting money, right?"
"Yes, ma'am," I say, expecting to be praised.
She stays not talking for a while,
kids are coming in the door banging to class.
She looks at me and she's making an equation in her head
that dawns.
I see her thinking I'm taking advantage of Jolly.
Inside my head I go WHAAAAAAAAAAAAAAAT?
And somebody in there is saying,
If Jolly's wages to you are your ticket not to end up like Jolly,
it's some kind of crooked thing you didn't think of till now.
And inside my head I go again, WHAAAAAAAAAAAAAAAAT?

I quick ask, in my regular voice, "Jolly gets back in school,
she gets Day Care free?
How does she get back in school?"
She gives me a phone number from her memory and says,
"Ask for Barbara."

I write the number on my hand
and all the time I'm wondering how it could be
that I'm taking advantage.
And the Steam teacher goes to run the circle discussion,
where today's topic is same as yesterday's, Boundaries,
and how you keep hold of them for safety
not to let them get out of control.
If you got hurt too bad when you were little
you don't know your boundaries good,
you could let people in too close & they hurt you
or you keep them way far away & they can't help you
and Steam Class is where you help figure it out.

39.

*B*ut Jolly won't call this Barbara.
So I do it. Inside me there's still this voice
asking if I'm stealing from Jolly.
Barbara answers the questions I think of
but I don't think of them all in time
before we hang up. I have to keep calling again.
By the time we finish we're old friends.

Barbara says the Day Care teaches
Respect for Little Ones.
What's that? Well, example,
they never go up behind Jeremy or somebody
and pick them up by the armpits.
That puts them at disadvantage,
they can't see who's coming. They always go around in front
like 'I'm picking you up now, see my familiar face?'
so not to ambush them.

Barbara tells me too about Jolly's classes.
She gets her rewards for
going regular. She gets office training,
she gets classes in child care,
she gets a nurse practitioner there all the time
to see Jeremy and Jilly stay well.
Her attendance has to stay regular
or she gets penalties.

Everybody in the program is either a mom
or pregnant to begin with,
trying to finish school.

I'm standing there on the phone taking in the details
that Barbara tells me
and I'm picturing a clean office
with maybe a geranium plant
and a smiling poster on the wall of babies or a puppy,
I'm writing things down like "Rspct f/Ltl 1's"
and "contrct *SIGN* hv to"
and I look over at Jolly and she's looking at the window
where somebody threw something last week and we taped
a Big Jake Frozen Clam Sticks With Carrots box
over the hole to keep the cold air out
and I imagine her making her eyes go empty that way
in front of the teachers at the Moms Up program
that Barbara is telling me about,
and I ask Barbara, I try to be casual,
"Uh, any special G.P.A. you have to have?"
hoping Jolly won't even remember such a word
from her past.
Barbara says in my ear,
"Why, no, honey, all you have to do is come over,
there's no exam of your skills,
you just have to let yourself be helped, that's all.
Just let yourself."

Barbara still thinks it's me,
even though I said it was for my friend.
"Shall I make an appointment then?" she says on the phone.
I take the dive. "Yes," I say, and we settle

on a week from Tuesday.
I give her Jolly's name and Jolly huffs out of the room
and goes turning on the water in the kitchen
to ignore what I'm doing
on the telephone.

40.

*J*olly she's holding her hands to the sides of her head the
    very next night
like she's keeping something from spilling out on the floor
and I ask her, of course.
I'm too young to understand, she tells me.
I'm a child, she tells me, this is too complicated for me.
I ask her again anyway
what's with her hands up there pressing.

She looks at me like it's useless to tell me
and she tells me:
"You know how the astronaut up there in space
he might have to go outside the rocket he's in?
Like to make repairs or something?
Like they radio him up there
from down in Florida, they say he's gotta go outside
and fix something?"
I never heard Jolly talk about space before, so I listen hard.
"Yeah," I say.
Jolly says, "Well, he's hooked by his cord.
Like a big belly-button cord.
Right?"
"Right," I say, agreeing. I'm not sure but I say right anyway.

"Well, spose the hatch closes while he's out there.
By an accident."
She's breathing in short little puffs now, like the air's thin.

"It cuts his cord. Slices it right off. He floats away."
She takes her hands down and they float out to her sides
slow, like clouds drifting apart.
"See? He floats out there. Just out there. You know?"
Her voice is sort of floating too. "Just out there, on and on."
She breathes out for a long time.

Then she starts again. "See, even if they wanted
to send somebody after him, they wouldn't know
where to look.
He ain't connected. See?

"And even if he wanted to fall down, he couldn't.
Ain't any gravity to do it.

"He's just out there.

"Nobody knows where.

"See how alone he is?"
Jolly stands in the middle of the floor
and her arms are out like floating away.

She looks at me and I'm still listening,
I'm waiting to hear what the rest of the story is. The point.
Jolly she looks at me now disgusted.
"I knew there ain't a single point to telling you," she says.
She sits down on the sofa
and I see the lights go out in her face.

41.

"You need yourself a job where you can dignify,"
I say to Jolly one day soon.
I hear my mother's voice coming out of my mouth
and I quick put a cork in it, instantly,
then I go on without her.
"I'm gonna help you, Jolly."

She looks at me,
saying in her eyes this was a wrong beginning
and I know it already:
Who am I 14 to tell her 17
"I'm gonna help you, Jolly"?

"You remember that Barbara I kept calling?
The one where moms go back to school?
You know what it's called?
It's called the Moms Up Program.
Up, Jolly. Up. You know?"
She's looking suspicious at me.
"It's like a school inside a school.
They're all moms in that program,
Or gonna be moms.

"Going to school is how you get a better kind of job,
this Barbara says.
Jeremy and Jilly get Day Care like you saw,
there's an appointment for Tuesday."

She looks at me with those eyes
and it's like she's a prisoner, resenting.
But like she knows they might have better food in prison
than where she's been.

Jolly don't like somebody putting her in a Program.
"Program. Program. Makes it sound like—"
She picks up a piece of bread crust from one of Jilly's picnics
that she's always having under a chair
or someplace that's last on
anybody's list of places to eat.
"Makes it sound like people looking over you all the time."
She dumps the crust in the sink.
"Makes it sound like a test."

42.

Jolly's still screaming, "No Welfare!"
She keeps saying if Welfare finds her name again
the state will take Jilly & Jeremy away,
she saw it happen before
to people she knew.

I argue and I argue,
telling her what this Barbara said on the phone,
then I put her on the phone with Barbara to tell her herself.
It's that if she's going to school
they'll help her keep her kids.
Going to school is how she gets
her sure rights to keep her kids.
This Barbara tells her, and I hear Jolly on the phone saying,
"Yeah" and "Yeah" and "I will" and "Yeah" and "I will."

And it's like Jolly's a little kid,
promising to be good. And I think how she said
she never remembered any real mom,
and I think how that real mom would hear her now, saying,
"Yeah" and "Yeah" and "I will" and "Yeah" and "I will."

43.

Jolly has the application, it says Department of Human
   Resources,
Adult & Family Services Division, it has 4 pages
and she can't read all the words
and she doesn't know how to answer their nosy questions
and she calls me at home, she tells my Mom a lie
saying it's about Jeremy's boots,
and my Mom is definitely not overjoyed when she's lied to.

"What's this question j. mean?
'Does everyone in your home buy and fix
their food together?'" Jolly wants to know.
"And this question i:
'Did anyone's entire income stop recently? Why?'"
I help her explain it doesn't mean
Jilly has to fix her own food,
it means are they a family over there at her house,
and she checks the Yes box for question j.
on the phone.
Jeremy wants to say hi
and after he says "Hi Bon" 3 times
he decides he just wants to listen,
so I sing him the song I made up,
"Rain is a puddle in my boot,
I'm an elephant with a rubber snoot,"
I made up the song when his cheap boot let water in.
I made it up so he wouldn't be so grouchy about it.

"What about question i.?
They say after, was it because 'job quit, layoff,
strike, etc.' Can I say it was a layoff?"
I don't know. I wasn't there in that closet and then got fired
for no reason at all
except being a magnet of bad luck like Jolly.
I tell her yes.
Then I tell her no.
She gets mad.
"Which is it then? What do I do? Nobody ever tells me.
Do you know there ain't a single person in the whole world
I can count on?
Do you know that? Not one single."

I know there's something wants saying
but I can't find it. She's there on the phone
doing her upset breathing
and behind her is Jilly hollering
and I tell her "Yes. Say layoff."
I don't know what to say.
A lawyer would know what to say,
all about Mr. Fingers Boss, but a lawyer is impossible.
Jolly can't pay a lawyer, she can't even pay me.

Jolly hangs herself up
with a click. My Mom stands there shaking her head
like it's all a complete shame.

part three

44.

So where Jolly goes to school is in the same building
but it's the Moms Up area.
Their classes are separate
with all different teachers.

They let you begin whenever. You get your own Day 1.
Jolly got herself and Jeremy and Jilly there on time,
I found out by Annie's sister in Day Care,
and Jolly was sitting in her class first thing,
even had a notebook and a pen
and her fingernails polished with Night Danger Red,
I heard.

I was proud I'd done part of the job
but not all of it. It was like I'd graduated from something.
But it was sad in a way,
like somebody took a chunk out somewhere
and didn't put it back.

My fourth-period teacher she asks me one day,
"Well, LaVaughn, you're getting more sleep these days?"
I tell her I guess so, and how does she know?
"You're quicker with answers, you raise your hand more.
It's noticeable," she says. "LaVaughn," she says,
"I want you to do yourself three favors
when you schedule for next fall.
One, get yourself into the Leadership Class.

It helps you find strategies for accomplishing things.
Two, sign up for the Financial Aid Seminar.
I think you need to go to college."

"Me too," I tell her. "I been wanting to go to it.
How did you know?"
She laughs looking me up and down.
"Your face, LaVaughn. It's in your face.
Behind your face, really. It's a discontent
with how things are. Even more of it lately."
Her voice gets very low now and she leans close.
"And I don't want to see you in this neighborhood
when I'm old and still teaching here." Then she thinks
and she says, almost whispering,
"Unless it's because you're a teacher too."

She now straightens up and pulls back and says,
"And Three,
take Grammar Build-Up.
It's second and third and fifth periods."
She sees me not wanting to do this.
"It won't kill you, LaVaughn.
And believe me, you need it. I have high hopes for you.
But your grammar frankly stinks."

She puts her arm around my shoulders to see if I'm insulted.
"You do those three things for yourself, LaVaughn.
You can thank me
when you graduate." I tell her OK
and I decide I can live with the insult.

45.

With Jolly back to school
and Jeremy and Jilly to Day Care
which Jeremy calls Day Dare
in his familiar voice,
I go back to the way I was before I ever even heard
of Jolly and her two kids that needed sitting.

My Mom is smacking her lips around the house
huffing that she never even saw
the inside of a Welfare office,
doesn't even know what bus stop you'd get off,
and eyeing my report card
like it's somebody's will and testament
and she's checking on what she got left in it.

She goes on about bootstraps
and I shut myself in my room
and I lay on my bed and I look at the ceiling
where there's the crack that partly looks like a tree
overhanging, the branch draping down.

I lay there and think how
I been sitting the kids free and that's not right.
But it is right.

Me sitting the kids free is like Jolly gets Welfare
right at home

from somebody almost a child herself, me.
And that's most definitely not right.
I should be paid for my services.
But then like it says Help Your Neighbor.
And like they say in Steam Class:
One good thing you do in a day for somebody else
don't cost you.
But then they go on about you have to find the good thing
that ain't the wrong good thing,
like for somebody going to abuse you,
or like you expect some big banquet of thanks for it
which you ain't going to get.
They make you give examples of both kinds.

So I end up not knowing
after I thought about it
no more than I did
in the first place.

46.

*G*uess what. Jolly got a B one day
and then three more B's
and then she did A work in typing
and she had all her columns lined up
on the what you call it the master list
and that made another A.
And her not being even in any school all those years.
At first she pretended it didn't make a difference
what grades she got
and then she changed her mind.

Just when she was adding up her A's and
you should see her prancing around
absolutely cool like she's a fancy princess—
Jeremy gets the chicken pox
and she stays home with him
and of course what happens to her school?
You guessed it.

So she misses 3 days till they call her on the phone
and they do some arranging
for Jeremy's chicken pox,
they arrange him a special place in Day Care
so he doesn't pox the others
and they say to Jolly,
"Why didn't you tell us the first day?"

And Jolly goes, "Well, nobody told me—I didn't know—"
She goes, "Nobody *told* me. You know?"

And when she says this
it's like a flat tire got fixed in my head
and I suddenly see the sign of her life: "Nobody told me."
I look in my brain and I make a brief list
of who's sposed to tell you things.
It's your folks
and your teachers
and your girlfriends
and your coach if you have a sport.

I look at Jolly
standing by the drinking fountain in B Hallway
where she still looks around like a foreign tourist
and I make inquiry in my mind.
Where's her folks? No sign of them ever since I knew her
and she won't answer questions about them if you ask.
And her teachers not even seen her
since before Jeremy and he's big.
And her girlfriends I notice she don't seem to mention.
And a sport?
I ask her, "Hey, Jolly, you ever play softball or soccer?
I mean used to once? Before?"

She looks at me like I was rude and she says,
"Here we got chicken pox and I had to miss school
and nobody ever tells me nothing and you want to know
did I ever play SOCCER?"
And she gives me her resentfulness
by saying that word.

"I just wondered, that's all," I say,
and I feel Jilly's forehead to see if she's hot,
trying to guess whether she's poxed yet.

Me and Jolly say Bye and I'll see you
and we go away in our separate directions.

47.

*T*hen one day when the poxes are gone off Jeremy,
one of the co-op counselers in the Moms Up Program
calls me out from my homeroom for a conference.
When I go there Jolly's there too
in the Moms Up counseling area
where it's screened off so they could make an office
where there wasn't one before,
and we say Hi like we just used to know each other,
like we used to ride the same bus.

So the counselor, this one that wanted the conference,
she leans her arms in red sweater sleeves on the desk
and she says, "Jolly and I were discussing
ways she can structure her time."
I try to picture Jolly saying "ways I can structure my time."
Jolly has her look on: she's gone into Underdrive.

"In your own words, Jolly, why don't you tell us
how you see the problem," the counselor says.
It isn't a question.
I see Jolly sifting through her list of problems
to find one she can even describe.
She moves her foot up and down,
swinging it across above the floor.
"Homework," she says.
"And how is homework a problem?" the counselor says.
Jolly looks at her. Jolly looks at me.

Jolly looks at her own hands
and she begins to pick at her fingernail,
the finger where she'd wear a wedding ring if she had one.
I suddenly imagine her being married
and having somebody to help her—
just even help change a diaper once in a while.

The counselor wants to explain for her.
"Homework is a problem for Jolly
because she's been out of school for some time,
and to reestablish a schedule is a challenge for her.
And the children keep her busy.
Isn't that right, Jolly?" says the counselor.
Jolly nods her head, Yeah.

"Jolly needs a Home Care Helper for a brief period;
we believe one hour each afternoon will be enough.
Our Sunshine Fund
can pay for a Home Care Helper in cases such as Jolly's,"
says the counselor. "With this help, Jolly will be able
to meet her homework responsibilities,
while the Home Care Helper
cares for the children," she says.

"However, Jolly and I see the matter rather differently,"
the counselor says, now she's talking to just me.
Jolly goes on picking her fingernail.
"Jolly wants you to be her Home Care Helper," she says.
"But we have a problem." She looks at me educational.
"You see, LaVaughn, you haven't been through
the Day Care Apprentice Program—"
and she starts listing

and pulling her fingers down backwards one at a time
with the other hand.
This is always fun to watch with teachers. It's not something
you'd want to do with your hands of your own free will.
"That's where we teach bathing the baby—"
she bends a finger backward,
"essentials of potty training—"
she forces the next finger down,
"communication with little ones,
meeting their safety needs—"
two fingers this time. I'm only listening and watching.
"Actually, we in the Program would prefer
that Jolly's Home Care Helper be someone we've certified
through our Apprentice Program."
Her fingers have flipped back natural now and she says,
"But I believe you've been caring for Jacky and Jeremy
for several weeks?
Jolly tells me they're very fond of you."

Now she's gotten to me. Coming at me with all those words,
and she don't know Jilly's right name,
and she wants me to get taught how to give Jilly a bath—
I get determined. My stomach gets determined.
I'm gonna take this job again. One hour.

But the counselor isn't finished.
Same time as Jolly is pronouncing
Jilly's right name to her,
the counselor is preferring again.
"We in the Program
must also be very sure
that the Home Care Helper's own academic work

won't suffer due to this added responsibility.
Are you doing average work, LaVaughn?
Of course we'll do an official check. But can you give me a—
just a general—"
And she puts out her hands to me like holding up two trays.

Then I do 3 things at the same time.
I tell her I'm doing good in school,
way far better than average.
I tell her I'd like to sit Jolly's kids again, one hour.
I let all my worry
about whether I was taking advantage of Jolly before
or whether she was taking advantage of me,
all that worry I let slide on out of my memory.
Me and Jolly are reconnected.

"My only concern is the question
of the Day Care Apprentice Program,"
says the counselor. She sits there thinking.
Jolly and me sit there with her.
The counselor says,
"See if you can fit it into your schedule in the fall.
All right, LaVaughn?"

And our conference is over. All the rest of the day
I notice I'm excited to be with the kids again.

48.

Myrtle and Annie were in agreement with my Mom by
   now:
I was definitely not in good company with Jolly.
"She don't sound like a good decision-maker."
This is Myrtle from her Steam Class.
"Those kids are adorable but their mother's all unorganized.
It's hard for kids that way to get good priorities."
This is Annie's report
from her sister in the Apprentice Program.

And me: being back with Jeremy and Jilly for one hour
was my vitamins I'd been not having.
One day me and Jeremy made
shadow pictures on the wall,
and we kept Jilly occupied
watching the ducks & chickens we made
and listening to them sing barn songs till she fell asleep.
And I repeated Jeremy's bed-making lessons also
which he had forgot. The hour went so fast
for a whole lot of days.

But Jolly: I watched her doing her homework sometimes
and her eyes go everywhere but on the paper.
She wants the TV on, even without the vertical hold,
just to listen to while she's doing her worksheets.

But then, who could expect work habits from somebody spent more time pregnant than she did in study halls?

49.

*M*e myself I made a giant mistake one day, and it's like
   this:
Jolly is quick with just-okay.
If it's not all the way done but partway
Jolly says that's good enough.
Dishes washed, always some left over,
2 math problems not finished at the bottom of the page,
garbage bag with a hole gashed in it so it spills.
Just part way is how come the high chair and the floor
are so disgusting.
I like things all the way done.
All the way is my ticket out of here
not to end up like Jolly.

One day I had it to my eyebrows with
partway-done. It's Jeremy's shirts this time,
damp in the drawer
and smelling you don't want to hear how bad.
"They been in here days," I say to Jolly.
"One day," she says back to me.
"One day on Jupiter," I say. "What am I gonna put on him?"

She finds a shirt in the dirty laundry and puts his arms in it,
she slides it over his face.
He goes off to do his boats in the bathtub.
I say to her—
and I'll be sorry till the day I die—

I say to her,
she's standing with the light from the bathroom
over her shoulder,
and in the background Jeremy's boats are sloshing,
I say to her, "That the way you did the birth control too?
Part way is good enough?"

Jolly got shorter faster than I could see
but I was an eyewitness and I know she did
just before she got taller,
layered with camouflage
and she could have held hand grenades.
Slowly she made her words come out,
and there was a weight there
I never heard before on anybody,
even soft as she was talking:
"Sometimes you don't have time.
Sometimes they don't let you have time to.
They get in a hurry,
they forget you're even around."
Jeremy hums boat-noises and splashes, I imagine his hands
sending boats on business
through the harbor in the bathroom.
Jolly's eyes go into remembering
and I begin to see what I've done.

Jolly says to me, "You're so perfect
what are you doing sitting my brats?
You're so highmighty
what are you doing even stepping in my door?
You're so expert in birth control
why are you going to school, you should be teaching it."

Jolly is saying, "You carry your schoolbooks
like they're some kind of Bibles,
you go to your classes, you pass your tests,
you smile all pretty at your teachers,
is that gonna make you never get pregnant
some guy gets you down where he wants you?"

In her excitement to say it all she's starting to yell
and her hair is shaking at me
and she says, "You come here just to make me feel like a
cockroach. LaVaaaawwwwnnnn. You come in here with your
homework, you got your Goals—" she says it sneering.
"You got your Cay-pa-bulls—" she says it to ridicule me.
"You're Miss Perfect and my kitchen floor is too *DIR-tee*
for you to walk on
and you tell me how *cuuuute* Jeremy rides the bus,
and you stole his toilet training,
you stole it from his own *mother*,
you have your little Jeremy-songs
you can make up out of your head,
you're such a good little mama I could PUKE."

These were her list of accusations.
I looked at her
in my hurry to find something to hit back with
and out came "You make excuses every time—"
and then two tears bounced down off her fist into the air
making puddles on her hand while I watched
and she's saying,
"And you bring your phony little lemon seeds,
they'll never bloom,
you're gonna break his heart!"

And she yells at me
"I'm not good enough for you,
go on home!"
I wonder if she means it
but I decide not to stick around.
I go to pass her
remembering where my math book is next to the door
and I go directly to my math book
not stopping to say Bye to Jeremy
or pick up Jilly who's hollering under a chair.
I'm leaving,
this place is too hot for me
and I'm sorry about the question I asked Jolly
that was none of my business
and my legs are shaking but I'm going anyway
and I bend down and scoop up my book fast

and then I do what I wasn't going to:
I turn my head and I look back.
On the floor in front of Jolly's foot
is a headless doll without clothes on,
its arm all twisted in a direction no person could ever reach
and beside her leg is her head
with happy plastic eyes staring dead at the ceiling.

I look at Jolly leaning on the wall
and her face is standing there
with those regretful eyes
and I'm just going to straighten that doll's arm
so I won't have to remember it every time I think of Jolly,
I'm just going to walk over and move the arm to normal
and I go to squat down at the bent doll

and Jolly's legs are standing in front of me
and my arms do the thinking
before I have time to check with them,
I'm hugging Jolly's legs
with both arms
and I'm telling her a lie, I'm saying,
"It'll be okay, Jolly. It'll be okay, Jolly. It'll be okay."

She caves in and boohoos hard, an avalanche of her voice
coming down her legs into my ears
and now I don't know what to do.
I was gonna leave, go study my math, study my English
not to end up like Jolly,
and here I am on the floor
holding her legs in my arms
and she sounds like a choir crying.

She slides down the wall
and now there are knees everywhere and she's gasping
and I'm locked in, looking in her face,
my math book is up against her leg,
and she begs,
kind of soft,
knocking my shoulder just a touch with her fist,
"Tell the time about your mother and the Vaseline,
come on. Tell about that time."
She looks like a promise,
like she can just begin living all over again from this minute
and everything will be fine.
"Come on, tell about that time," she says.

I shrug my shoulders and I start slow.
I tell her again the story she already knew
about my mother and her three friends
how they put Vaseline on their eyebrows,
their moms and my Mom's aunts
wouldn't let them wear makeup,
but Vaseline would make their eyebrows shine.
(Who wants shiny eyebrows? Jolly and me used to ask
when I told it before.)
And then about the four boys they knew
that took them to the drag races
and they were sposed to sit up on top of the Chevy
parked by the track
and watch the race
and the dust came like ocean waves
with every time the cars came around the laps,
and my mother and her three friends
looked like they had beards growing
on their foreheads, layers of dust piled on like frosting
stuck to the Vaseline
and the boys laughed so hard with shock
they never took those girls anywhere ever again,
not even to a movie.

And Jolly and me we imagine
the picture of four girls with eight beards
growing out of their foreheads
sitting on top of a Chevy somewhere back in history,
and we laugh like always.
I never can tell the story but we bust up laughing
at those four old-fashioned girls.

Jolly and me we laugh so hard this time
we bump heads, and Jolly picks up the naked headless doll,
kind of sways it back and forth,
and she turns the plastic arm back straight,
it squeaks a little,
and Jolly and me sit on the floor and look at each other
and listen for just an instant to Jilly still hollering
and Jeremy's boat song
and we both wish in our eyes
we had those girls' dumbness and ridiculous beards.

50.

*T*hat was the very first day Jilly crawled all the way across
   the floor.
She found her way out from under the chair,
came crawling all the distance
and she had floor fuzz on her mouth
and she ended up with her big eyes going uphill
at her mother
who had laughed her head off about the Vaseline beards
and her jeans were spotted wet with tears from being mad
and here's this little messy kid
who you think is a hopeless case
and she comes crawling and she plants herself
among us,
asking with her eyes,
What's up?

I thought about how I was blaming Jolly
for having Jilly when she should know better,
and then here comes Jilly on her own steam
all the way across the floor
to land here like a boat nobody expected.

There's just an instant
where she's looking up at Jolly
and the floor fuzz on her mouth puffs out in curls
when she breathes
and nobody says anything

and everything is flat quiet
except for Jeremy going "Brrrmmm, Brrrmmm"
with his bathroom boats,
and Jilly's hands are on the floor like animal feet,
looking so primitive
like she lived in a cave.

Then Jolly picks up Jilly
and holds her tight against her chest
with Jilly's feet sticking out of her half-off socks
and I pick myself up off the floor
and I say I'll see you Friday,
and I close the door behind me
and I go down the stairs because their elevator is broke
and I walk through the potato-chip bags to the bus stop
and I don't know what I know
but I know
I know something I didn't know before
and I get on the bus
and I don't feel any different
but it's like I have 2 minds, one I'm riding home on the bus
and the other I'm back there looking at Jilly and her mother
like they had different faces,
like they're people I never saw before
sitting there on the floor
clinging with everything they got.

51.

*N*ow they're wondering at Day Dare
why Mr. Jeremy won't pick up the macaroni pieces
to glue on the card
to make pictures
but he'll do other activities,
and you should see his paintings.
They're like some modern artist
that puts paint on with a broom,
they're that big.

But he won't play their puzzles
and he knocks his cup off the table too many times
in their opinion. Mr. Jeremy is a problem
they say.
I'm thinking it's his home surroundings
how it's like at his house:
it's like somebody standing on one foot
and wobbling all the time
waiting to catch a right balance.

But the Day Dare people have other things on their mind.
They want to give him an exam.
"Exam what?" says Jolly to me.
"He's sposed to know answers?"
She's mad and starting to lift her voice.
They tell her they mean an exam of his coordination
and his eyes. So Jolly takes him to the doctor

where they tell her to,
and she tells me how he has to sit in the chair with the lights
and the green spot with the moving dot on it
and they find out—

"Oh, no," says Jolly,
"How come this happened?" she says.
"Jeremy, this is too much," she says to him.
And she's looking around the room
to find somebody to blame it on
because they find out Jeremy can't see right
when it's close up
and he needs glasses.

To tell the truth, I know what Jolly means.
You know how much glasses cost?
Just to think about it
makes Jolly want to go to bed and pull the blanket up
all over herself, she says.
She's all in her Jeremy-how-could-you? mood
that I know from my house. Mothers go
How-could-you? when you start costing them money.
It's in Mom School they learn it
before they got born. Even accidental moms like Jolly.

So Jolly takes a few days to go Jeremy-how-could-you?
and then she gets around
to keeping the appointment they made.
And Jeremy has "Gas," he calls them, the glasses.
This is cute or not,
depending on how your mood is when you have to go
putting them on him

or how many times he forgets where they are
or how he complains
when you put the harness around his head
to keep them from falling off.

Now a kid with glasses is a different kid.
He's more expensive.
He's more breakable.
He's more on your mind all the time.

And his eyes, they look so big they're scary,
like he can see too much,
so you don't just go around him the way you would.
You go around careful
because of all the things being pulled in
by his big deep eyes.

And Jilly grabs for the Gas
and Jeremy hits her
and Jolly yells how she can't study her bookkeeping
with the hollering
and it's life like before in the continent of I don't know what
but it's different.
Because of the glasses. Because of the Gas.

His eyes are so huge when he looks at you.
So huge.

52.

When she finds out Public Assistance
is paying for the Gas
wouldn't you think Jolly'd be happy?
Nope. She hates everything about it.
"Welfare!" she still says
like it's a dirty diaper from some drug addict's baby,
a filthy thing she don't want in her house.

I think she has my Mom's voice in her memory:
"You need to take hold, girl."
I can't make excuses for my Mom.
Truth is, moms don't wait to hear explanations.
They go making their sermons first.
It's another rule they learn in Mom School.

Jolly's thinking if Public Assistance pays for the Gas
she's not taking hold.
I'm thinking if Public Assistance pays for the Gas
Jolly has that much more of her attention
she can pay to her schoolwork
and she has that much less she has to pay to
getting some bad-wage job
where she can't dignify.

I say this to her
and she goes moping into the kitchen and
washes the dishes so she won't have to argue with me.

And I notice something right under my nose:
The dishes are stacked neat and orderly,
the counter doesn't have yuck in the cracks,
no cereal is all over the high-chair edges.
The floor is still terrible, though.

I look at Jolly running hot water into the suds
and I lean around her shoulder into her face
and I say to her, "You'll make it, Jolly."
And she shrugs her shoulders
and I have a feeling like her shoulders and mine are joined
some way.

So around the corner comes Jeremy
with his deep-sea eyes
and Jilly crawling fast behind him
and Jeremy says to me like a grouch but wondering,
"No lemon blom."
And all my good feeling goes curled up at the edges
like with mold
and I feel guilty
about the lemon tree Jeremy doesn't have.

53.

So I say to my Mom I ain't got my social studies done yet
    one morning
when she's shoving oatmeal at me across the table
and a spoon.
Very early in the morning,
she gives me her "All right, I've absolutely had it" look
that usually a mom should save for later in the day.

"You *what*?" she's saying, like a judge,
all she's missing is the gavel
to pound the table with.
I tell her, "I'll do it, I got Break before Fourth."
The oatmeal steams.

"No," she says. "You back up a little,
back there to what you just said."
I repeat myself about the social studies.

My Mom adds five pounds across her chest
by breathing in deep
and she says to me very clear:
"Nobody says AIN'T in this house.
Nobody ever said that word here before.
Nobody needs to say that word here now.
You know why, Miss?
Miss, you know why?"
And she gives me a little bit of room to answer.

Like in school, they ask a question,
they have in mind only one right way to reply.
A whole room full of brains
but they'll only pick one being right.
"I'll tell you why, and you don't forget," she announces.
"You say AIN'T on the job,
your boss gets nervous.
Your boss gets insecure when you talk like that.
Your boss thinks he's got stupid people working there.
He gets afraid.
Your boss gets nervous, insecure, he gets
afraid,
next thing you know you get passed over
or maybe fired.
Then who pays the rent?"

She lets this sink in.
Then comes the next part.
"You think people in college say AIN'T?
You say AIN'T, they'll send you right back home.
Then what'll I do with you?"
She also lets this sink in.

"So. Now. You tell me your social studies," she says.
I'm eating oatmeal, blowing on each bite first.
There is completely no point
in arguing with this woman
on this subject.

"I haven't got it done yet," I say.
She gets softer, she gets soothing.
"You gonna do it at Break?"

"Yeah," I tell her.

"That's my girl," she says,

and she turns around rinsing the oatmeal pan in the sink.

"It's that Jolly," she mutters. I let her tell it to the faucet.

54.

"That billionaire!" says Jolly one day
when I arrive for my just one hour of sitting.
She's got the rent bill in her hand
and I see waving up and down it says
3 months back she hasn't paid.
"The one in the newspaper,
he gives it away,
just if you ask
and you're deserving,
that's all you need. He gives it away."

I remember the one she means.
He gives his billions in portions
to people they need false teeth or a wheelchair
and you see him in the newspaper.
They write him letters
and he tells them in the paper
right to their faces
if he gave them the money they want
or if he turned them down.
Some of them aren't deserving enough.

I don't understand how this billionaire
isn't the Welfare she hates.
I say to her, "One's giving and the other's giving too,
so what's the difference?"
And she says to me like I'm stupid:

"For him you have to be deserving."
This is her argument.

She has to write a business letter
for her business class in the Moms Up Program,
and she figures this letter to the billionaire in the newspaper
is her business letter,
and she works on it the whole time I'm there for my one hour
while I play Lego blocks with Jeremy and clean up after Jilly
who is crawling everywhere now
and investigates behind the toilet like an inspector.

I been fired for no good reson
and my kids one has to have glasses he goes to Day Care
and I been back to school
so I get better job then
could you give me some of the money for this rent
so they kick us out on the street
I and my kids Jeremy and Jilly am deserving you will see.

She shows me this letter.
I feel bad knowing her words when she doesn't.
Handing me the letter
she has her look on. Her look says:
"Tell me I done it right so I don't have to change it,
I don't know how to."
She does it with her accounting and her geography, too.

I maybe could just not tell her at all
but there's that one word she left out,
the letter don't make sense if she don't put it in there
where it goes.

So they kick us out on the street it isn't what she meant.
If I don't say nothing about it
the teacher will tell her when she turns it in
for her business-letter credit.

Then I see her she's making a neat copy
all straight on the margins.
So I ask to make sure: "You handing this letter in for credit?
Or you gonna mail this one to the newspaper?"
"I donknow," she is shrugging.
I roll around a carrot that's lying on the floor
with my foot.
Then I think I'll wait to see
if she catches the missing word herself.
I go away from her chair and then come back.
And she didn't catch it and she wrote the same mistake.
I tell her, "Jolly, you mean to put 'don't' in that place."
I point to it.
She looks.
"So they put us. So they put us on the street.
So they don't put us on the street." She's reading out loud.
"I put it in the first time," she says.
I don't say anything. She's hunting in her first paper.
"No. It ain't even there," she says.
She takes a little breath to get good and mad at this one.

But there's too many people to get mad at,
and I can see her circling around
trying to aim at the right one.
On her posture it's written: "Nobody told me."

And then Jolly she does an unusual thing.
What she does is sit still and push the neat margin paper
away from her on the table.
The first one she takes
and puts in the word "don't" sideways.
Then she gets herself a clean piece of paper
and she starts in again right up at the top,
the date and the address and all, and what's so odd is:
She does all this regular, not grouchy or squinty-eyed angry,
she just does it.
I don't know how she fixed the blame for the mistake.
I go away to brush Jilly's hair
and when I come back the letter's finished.
All done like Jolly wants it,
no missing words.

Jolly she just did it.
I wanted to cheer like those cheerleaders you see
at the games.
But instead I made wrinkly faces with Jilly
for Jilly's attention span,
which is short. About six faces is all.

Then Jeremy gave me 5 for Good-bye
and I went home.

55.

All the time Jolly kept insisting she was nobody's kid, ever.
"No, I don't have folks, I told you," she told me.
Better not push, her face read to me.
She says she slept in a refrigerator box when she was 12
and got her period she didn't know what it was,
thought she was insane or dying,
some lady took her to the Girls' and showed her what to do.
A Sister Saint Somebody. She explained it to Jolly,
told her she was normal,
not dying.

But when Sister Saint Somebody went to get the papers
to fill out Jolly's name on them, Jolly thought
she meant to put her in one of those orphanages
like they have for people without folks,
so she walked.

"But I had the Maxi-pad things in a bag she gave me,
so I could get on the bus just like anybody.
You know, I looked around
and I looked around
and I said every single lady and girl has this
if Sister Saint Somebody was right.
I counted 17 ladies and girls on the bus.
And I thought of all the blood.
That's a lot of blood. You know?"

And I say Yes, that's a lot of blood.
"You ever wonder about the ones in refugee places?
I mean in other countries?" I ask Jolly.
Sure, she wonders, she says.
Those ladies in the mountains,
those ones that wear the hoods.
And those ladies in the African nations
all starving with their babies
so skinny they'll die
before the food packages land from the helicopters.

All that blood, me and Jolly wonder together.
Where does it all go?
A whole ocean of blood.
All those thousands of years
all the ladies and girls been bleeding.
Where would it all be?
In the ground someplace.

Me and Jolly are quiet for a long time,
then she's laughing and laughing, I think she's gonna choke.
She gathers in her breath and she says to me,
all sort of serious, like she's making a report to the class,
"That's why they call her Mother Earth."

And she gets up off the sofa
and whirlies of sponge rubber fly up behind her
and she goes to get her notebook. She has a notebook now,
it's a 3-ring, just like regular school students,
she carries it like it's not a habit yet.
It fits different in her arm,
not like it was always there.

She goes and gets it because she's sposed to write a report
on Peru.
I ask her if she's gonna say where all the blood
from the Peru women goes.
She sticks out her tongue
and puts her pen into her hair
and stares at the clean page in the notebook.
"What I'm gonna say on Peru?" she says.
"Start with the exports," I tell her.
"No, start with the population.
No, start with the food.
That's a good place to start," I tell her.
"No, start with the mountains.
Or the beach, they have a nice beach there."

Now she gives me her look.
"Nobody helps me the right way," she complains very loud.
"Everybody tries to confuse. How you ever sposed to learn
if nobody does nothing but confusion
all the time?" she says.

But I'm remembering just the other day
she corrected her mistake in that billionaire letter
so I just go and pick up Jilly to change her
and ignore Jolly
singing that old song again.

56.

"*I* had a Gram, though," Jolly says,
out of the blue completely.
We're waiting for Jeremy to finish pooping in the toilet
so we can go to the dryer with quarters.
"A gram of what?" I ask her, not wanting to know.
There's drugs all around the neighborhood
but this Jolly always far as I know is
keeping herself clean
because of what she told me once:
She was pregnant with Jilly
before she could even collect her thoughts.
That's what she said:
"Before I could even collect my thoughts.
Don't never go near that drug.
It gets you pregnant faster than anything."
I looked at her. Was she dumb or something?
"You go smoking that drug,
it goes straight down inside your underwear,
it makes no stops in between.
You end up pregnant
because some guy has some nice high for you."
I look at her some more.
"It's what you call an afro Deez," she says.
She says, "Some nice high:
you're throwing up your breakfast all the time
and then you have some baby
their father is off the face of the earth

154

like magic."
I look at her some more.

"That drug makes women pregnant,
it makes men disappear. It's a magic drug."

Now, weeks later, when she suddenly says "Gram,"
she explains: "I mean a big-G Gram,
a lady took care of me," she says this time.
"Put me back together all the time.
Hugged me, preached to me, put me in bed,
played double solitaire.
That kind of a Gram.
She put me a vitamin pill on the table every breakfast.
She had socks clean in the drawer for me,
my own towel."

"Then you have folks," I said to Jolly who always said before
that there wasn't any.
It's to get the story straight I say it.
Not to accuse her.

She looks away from me
down at a cockroach on the floor edge.
"Not anymore," she says. She keeps looking at that roach.
"She's dead," she says. "What she used to do most
was comb.
And she brushed, too. She had this big brown comb
and a blue one.
And a yellow one, that was for the cats.
And when she brushed my hair
she always talked about her garden.

She talked about her beans.
Then her what you call 'em dahlias.
And she brushed with a great big black brush,
and she'd go on
about how I was sposed to pick the peas clean.
I wasn't sposed to leave any.
Big black brush and her garden, and she smelled like lotion,
that kind in the yellow squeeze bottle."

Jeremy finished and we get ourselves out the door,
in our parade of people carrying quarters
jingling down the stairs.
The elevator's broke like always
and you don't want to go to the laundry room alone
in Jolly's building, ever. You go together.

And while Jolly is going on
about the clean way her Gram smelled
and all about the combing of the cats,
even the fur details of the cats, how one was striped and one
had an odd unmatching whisker another color,
this is where I found out
how she came to call Jeremy his name.

"And he was there in the kitchen
with a cookie hangin' in his hand
and laughing. He laughed and he laughed,
and he used to call me Minnie Mouse.
He wore this yellow necktie
like you never see
and he always brought bananas, every time," says Jolly.

"Who was this again?" I ask. Truly my mind drifted,
it was too many cats to listen to. We're tossing clothes
in the dryers and Jeremy's helping,
carrying one sock at a time.

"I said it was one of Gram's *other* foster kids
that wore the yellow necktie.
He was all grown-up, he still came back to visit.
He rototilled.
And we always had that shaky red Jell-O salad
when he came, along with maybe roast.
Or chops. And gravy. He laughed and laughed
and he had a bag of bananas.
He'd be on a chair holding one of the cats in his lap
curled up asleep
and he'd call me Minnie Mouse."

"He what?" I say. "He roto-what, this grown-up foster?"
"He roto*tilled*," says Jolly, "and his name was Jeremy."
Me, I'm listening to this discovered name of her little son.
So that's where she got it.
From a time when she had some kind of folks.
Or something like folks.
Red shaky Jell-O salad
and they laughed in the kitchen
and he wore a yellow necktie.
"It's for the garden, it's a machine.
It turns the soil. So you can plant. You have to rototill.
Otherwise nothing grows."

Jilly sets up a wail when Jeremy slams the dryer door.

Now Jolly turns out to know about gardens
and rototillers, out of her past
which isn't a complete blank mystery anymore.
"But she died," Jolly says.
I tell Jolly I'm sorry she died,
and we start up the laundry stairs.
"She had a family-tree T-shirt,
all the names sewed on it all over,
all her foster kids, there was eleven.
I was on it. She sewed my name in pink," Jolly says,
and she wipes some green ick off Jilly's nose with a diaper.
Jolly has a different voice on, now, remembering.
She goes slow.
We're walking up the stairs
and Jeremy's doing his march, holding my hand.

"He was the nicest man, that one," says Jolly.
"Always folded his towel
after he washed his hands in the kitchen
after he rototilled the garden," Jolly says.
Then she's quiet some more. Then she starts up again,
"And he always brought bananas.

"And Gram said to me, she said,
'Now you come back to see me too,
just the way Jeremy does.
You do that, Jolly. Don't you never forget your Gram.'
And she laughed
and brushed her cats.
But she died,
so I couldn't go back and see her, ever."

And then we're back at the apartment
and my one hour is up
and Jolly never says anything more
about these folks that used to be,
ever again.

part four

57.

In one of her classes Jolly's sposed to swim
and she's sposed to take Jilly along too.
Jeremy has a swimming class with his age.
Picture this Jolly and her baby
and the other Moms Up and theirs
and they're screaming in the pool together
and getting instructions
how to not drown
because of course Jolly and the Moms Up are all
gonna live in Palm Springs
with their own pools and their butlers.
That's what they say,
"Yeah, this is for when I get the pool and the butler."

Really it's just the Red Cross like always.
"We been teaching people to swim since 1914," they say.
It's on Jolly's written test, the date when.
The Moms Up school gives Jolly graduation credits
for swimming lessons
and she needs all the credits she can get.

What she has to do, Jolly,
besides learn to put her face in water and swim
is she has to learn the CPR
because she's a mom
and they won't let her graduate without it.
It's how you save somebody's life.

So now for her homework
Jolly has to do accounting and geography
and nutrition and math and then she does her
Family Interrelationships
and Dynamic Awareness worksheets
and her Child Safety Study Sheet.
So she has me quiz her and
pretty soon we both know
what the carotid and brachial pulses are
in a little kid
that you feel for when they get hurt.

And while she's doing her homework
there's Jeremy looking
like up from under water in his glasses
and Jilly always tells you where she is by her talking.
Her talking is "Gaa" and "Gaa" and "Baa" and
"Mlpwulmwlpmmm"
so she never gets lost behind the bed
or somewhere
without letting you know.

58.

*A*nd Jolly has to know her kids' favorite food also. This is
   for her math.
Because she has to then do her Estimating homework.
With Jilly it's simple. It's that mix-butterscotch pudding
that a lot of it would frankly
make you throw up. Jilly eats it and won't stop.
Picture what it's like when she gets an upset stomach,
don't ask.

With Jeremy it's harder
'cause he likes so many things,
things they gave him new at Day Dare
he never had before.
They give him raw zucchini, it's good for him. And jicama
and rhubarb crumble.
But what he likes most is probably
Hershey's Kisses. So Jolly she's sposed to Estimate
how many he'll eat in his life.
She has to know how many weeks in a year.
And how many he'll eat in a week,
including she has to average in
the weeks he won't have any.
Then she has to decide how many years he'll be
actively eating Hershey's Kisses. "Actively eating,"
that's what the worksheet says.
"Actively eating, what's that?" Jolly says.

I look at it & tell her I guess it's he's taking interest
in his eating.
"What?" she says.
"He would be eating chocolate without taking interest?
Who would?"
And I notice,
like I noticed before sometimes,
this: When we have a Situation
as they call it in Steam Class
me and Jolly we laugh.
And I notice more too:
it ain't what—isn't what—I do that makes it funny,
me that goes to school all the time
and does the work assigned.
No, it's that Jolly, what she does.
She's the one makes it funny, the Situation.

Here's the example:
If math credits equaled money, she wouldn't have enough
to barely buy a bus token;
add to that,
not only 1 but 2 guys got her so confused she got pregnant;
add to that, she doesn't have folks;
and she's in Remedial on Thursdays,
an added insult to her reading;
she thinks that billionaire in the newspaper
is gonna pay her rent,
she even mailed him the letter.
And yet here she is
saying nobody eats chocolate without interest
and the math paper doesn't know it's so hilarious
but Jolly does.

I look at her and I notice her way of taking hold.
It isn't my Mom's way
but it's a way.
Maybe it ain't a way to get her out of here.
But it's a way.

I don't know. The way Jolly makes a joke out of a Situation
maybe is the wrong way.
Or maybe it's the right way.

Jolly sees me looking at her studying
and she asks me what it is on my mind.
"Somethin' here makin' you stare,
maybe I'm a movie?" she says.
I decide not to tell her.
"No," I say. "My hour's up," I say.

I don't want to tell her I'm thinking
how she's got things so stacked up against her
and yet she gets a laugh out of her math worksheet.

"But how many years Jeremy gonna eat all them kisses?"
she's asking.
We look at him, he's at the window,
picking in the dirt where no lemon is.

Jolly says to him,
"Jeremy, how old you gonna be
when you don't like Hershey's Kisses?"
He don't turn around.
He sings, "Lemon blom, lemon blom," it's his song.
There's no sound except his voice singing to a pot of dirt

and Jolly—I look at her,
her face empties out of all the math she was thinking about
and she says, so suddenly slow and soft:
"Jeremy will die someday."
She looks down with those eyes of hers and she says,
"He's just regular.
Just a person."
She remembers I'm there and she looks at me
like I can solve that.
I'm remembering back to the day she said the astronaut
all unhooked from his ship
was so alone, I'm remembering the way
her arms floated out sideways
drifting, going nowhere.
"You know that?" she asks me, hushed,
Jeremy shouldn't hear.

And it's so silent in that room with just us breathing
I don't know what to say
and I don't say anything,
there not being any words
for what Jolly knows and I know and Jeremy don't.

59.

So one day Jolly meets me like usual after school
for just my one hour,
and I know already it's gonna be longer.
It's her face. It's her teacher in the Parent Skills Class.
Now Jolly never got excited in liking a teacher before,
I know for a fact. So I listen close.

"She told this story, it was about a blind lady
somewhere over there in a country,
one of the far ones
where they don't have health."

I listen on.
"This lady's blind and she's poor
and she washes people's laundry on the rocks,
you know, in the river, the way they do in those places.
And she has these kids that are in starvation
and the blind lady she goes out with her old cane
thumping on the hard dirt of the town,
she's goin' out shopping, she wants an orange
for her kids, to get the vitamins.
She has enough money to buy one orange.
She'll divide it for her kids.
From washing the laundry, she has the money.

"So she goes to the street where they have the market,
all busy with donkeys and everything in the way.

And she nearly gets knocked over by some bad boys
but she gets to the fruit market
and she smells all the fruits
and she just wants one best orange
for her children.
So she holds some oranges in her hand
and she finds the best one.
Even being blind, she can smell how juicy it is,
and she pays her last money for the orange
and starts thumping home
with her cane.

"What happens on the way home is
the same bad boys from before,
they trip her and she falls and drops the orange.
Her nose is bleeding from her falling
and she's reaching across the ground
for her cane and she's a mess.
So one of the boys
says how he's so sorry to see her in the dirt,
he tells her he was just passing by and saw her fall.
She knows this is a lie
but he's handing her back her orange,
and he even hands her her cane.
So she thanks him and she gets up and thumps on home;
now she's bleeding from her nose but she's on her way home
to her starving children.

"But with her bleeding nose she couldn't smell
so she doesn't know till later what that boy done.
She gets home and guess what?"
I tell Jolly I don't know what.

"Guess," Jolly is insisting.
"I don't know," I tell her. "The lady's bled all to death."

"No," Jolly says. "It's her orange for the children.
She ain't got it.
She cuts it open and the bad boy cheated her,
he gave her a lemon,
not no orange. She smells this sour lemon smell
coming up from the fruit she cut
and she's mad."

"So?" I say.

"So. First you know what she does?
First she tells herself how stupid she is, she should know
the very instant he gave it to her.
Should have figured it was a lemon."

"That's what I was thinking," I say.

Jolly she looks at me.
"Remember how she was when he put it in her hand?"
This is now
one of those tests in school where you read the paragraph
and they ask questions after.
"She was fallen down in the dirt, bleeding," I say.
"She couldn't smell."
"Well?" says Jolly, hard-voiced.
"She still should've felt it careful
to know it was smaller than an orange," I say.
Jolly looks at me accusing.
"That's what they always say," she says.

"They always say,
'You should've *known* you was getting a lemon.' "
She exaggerates her voice.

I begin to get the picture.
"But you don't always know at first," Jolly says.
"You even thank them for it most of the time. See?
See how they get you when you're down,
you don't even know it's a lemon."
She's building up steam, this Jolly is.
"You even *thank* them for it,
and you go stumblin' home,
all bleeding or however you're hurt—
and you say to yourself,
    'Well, gosh, I guess somebody give me a lemon.
    Ain't I stupid.
    Ain't I dumb. I must've deserved it
    if I was so stupid not to know."

And Jolly looks at me,
angry because she understands.

"So. This is the next part of the story. Guess what
the blind woman does next.
Guess," she goes on at me.
This Jolly she's excited now.

I tell Jolly I don't know. I say,
"Her children are all hungry, she's blind,
she's got just this one lemon,
I don't even like this story, Jolly.
Why're you telling it?"

"For the *point* of it," she says.
"You know what she does next?
She finds this little teensy bit of old caked, lumpy sugar
she had packed away, and she mixes it up
with the juice of the lemon
and some clean water from the spring they have there,
and she makes lemonade.
And she feeds it to her starving little ones.
And that's the end of the story.
That's the point of it."

And I get the point of it this time.

And I want to put my arms all the way around Jolly
in congratulation
and I'm happy she's so angry
and I'm proud of her
she made it clearer than my Mom ever did
with all the preaching and huffing
and bootstraps.

But I hold back. I don't go hugging Jolly.
She's too angry to hug.
It's like some bricks got fit in the wall
where it was crumbly before.

And that's the day Jilly chooses—
it's like she just lay there on the floor and chose—
she up and walks.
Jolly and me we're being mad together in the kitchen
and Jolly's picking up the mess of banana
that Mr. Jeremy left on a chair,

and up comes Jilly
on her two feet
looking like somebody on a boat deck,
with her surprised face
not knowing whether she's gonna fall down
or fly.

60.

I'm remotivated, like they say in Steam Class.
Got a power surge, like they say.
I'm gonna teach Mr. Jeremy his numbers,
you know why?
He says Jilly took 11 steps
but it can't be that many, she's too lurchy.
"Leben," he says. So we count.
"How many fingers?" I say to him. I hold up 3.
"9," he says, and he looks at me
out of those deep glasses he wears.
"How many spoons?" I say.
"9," he holds 2 in his hand.
I take hold of his 2 feet. "How many?" I quiz him.
"Leben," he's so sure.

This Mr. Jeremy, he's imagining things.
"No, 2," I say.
"1," I grab his left foot.
"2," I grab his right.
"9, Leben," he answers me, grabbing my feet right back.

I don't give up.
"You want 9, I'll give you 9," I offer him. I fill a whole page
from my social studies notebook with 9's.
These 9's they have faces, and hands and feet,
they're a whole family of 9's all over the page.
"Now you color these 9's," I say,

and I serve him the box of crayons
and run over to where Jilly's turning on the stove burner,
her new hobby.

I continue with Jeremy's numbers
because I don't want his ignorance to beat me.
"1 belly button," I count on him. "And 1 on your sister,"
I count on her.
"1 blue crayon," I hold up in his face.
"2 ears," I go on his head.
"And 2 hands, 2 feet," I continue down him.
Wearing his glasses he looks like he understands.

But when I ask him again
he tells me he has eleven feet
and a belly button.

He pretends he's a lost cause.
I go into my bag from home and I pull out his surprise.
I open the paper towel. "7 new lemon seeds," I tell him.
"And 1 part of a bag of potting soil.
And 1 little bunch of fertilizer and plant food," I tell him.
And together we make the pot of old dead nothing
into a new garden of future lemon trees
plus 4 orange seeds from Day Dare.

Mr. Jeremy looks at me somewhat suspicious.
He has a right, it didn't work before.
"It's potting soil," I tell him.
"Things will be different this time."
And I almost shake my head,
for all the times people will say that

in his disappointed life to come. But Mr. Jeremy decides
to give me 5 anyway. We slap each other 5
for old times' sake.

61.

*J*olly's watching the mail.
And she goes to the neighbors for their newspaper
that smells like cigarettes from their place.
She wants to see when the billionaire pays her rent.
I'd be embarrassed, but Jolly she's not.
She's at a brink all the time anyway,
I guess she figures getting her Situation in the news
ain't the worst.
I don't think he'll answer her.

Now that Jolly knows about the blind lady and the lemon,
and walking rules ain't familiar to Jilly
but she walks anyway,
and Jeremy looks everywhere
out of those pools his glasses make,
and Jolly keeps on doing her homework most of the time,
and they're back and forth to school and Day Care—
things don't feel so falling apart around here.

I look around,
across the trail of things Jilly's pulled out of drawers
and still the same stuck jam on the rug from so long ago
even the ants don't like it anymore—
and I think how things could be getting worse
but they're not.
It's like a plug got stuck in the sinking ship or something.

And I look over at Jolly winding her hair around her finger
and doing her homework for health
with a regular ballpoint pen
and regular spiral paper
and I don't see how that billionaire could take notice
if he didn't come here and see for himself.
How would you know,
if you didn't see the way things were before?

How would you know things ain't—aren't—getting worse?
How would you be able to tell
people are trying hard around here?
You'd have to see for yourself.

I'm thinking about this when Mr. Jeremy comes running,
carrying his book about the crab,
it's open to a page of 3 fish neighbors,
he slaps me 5,
and tells me, "Leben fish here, right?"

And what happens is this, in a private letter to her house:
To the mother of Jeremy and Jill:

*I am pleased to hear that you are studying to complete
your graduation equivalency requirements. When you are able
to demonstrate your sincerity by sending me a copy of your
G.E.D. certificate, your tenacity will be rewarded with a check.*

*In the meanwhile, allow me to pay my respects to your
determination.*

Enclosed is my small check for a treat for Jeremy and Jill.

And a five-dollar check slides out of the envelope.
Jolly she doesn't know if she's mad or happy
at this billionaire.

Meanwhile, I'm surprised in astonishment.
He actually reads his mail and he answers it.
All those letters in the newspaper ain't—aren't—made up
in his office
just to get attention.

Me and Jolly we don't know what "tenacity" is
but we're both glad it will be rewarded.

"Your tenacity will be rewarded," we say to each other
and we make billionaire faces.
And she makes a billionaire speech,
holding her toothbrush up for a mustache:
"We ain't gonna reward
your little eensy one-a-city, two-a-city,
we're gonna save it all up
and reward your ten-a-city when you get it."

62.

And then there's me.
I'm supposed to take
all those different classes:
that Financial Aid one,
that Leadership one,
and Grammar Build-Up,
and I can go to college to be a teacher. Really?
Yeah. Me.

And then there's the what did she call it?
The one Annie's sister is in.
Day Care Apprentice Program, where they teach you
communication with little ones.
My grammar may frankly stink but me and Jeremy
know what we mean.

There's no class to teach me communication with dead ones.
That's what I want.
I want to talk to my Dad. One conversation. That's all. One.
I want to ask him if we'd still be living the same place
if he was alive.
I want to ask him
did he love my mother when they had me.
I mean love her to stay with her her whole life if he could of.
I want to ask him would he help me pay for college
if he could come back alive.
I want to ask him should I be a teacher.

I want to ask him will things turn out okay.
Is that too much to ask?

I don't want to ask him how bad it hurt.
I don't want to know that.

63.

What I'll never forget
when I'm long gone out of here
and this place is all torn down with a bulldozer—
What I'll never forget—
It was the sound in Jolly's voice when she said
that one word to Jilly.

It was only the fault of Jilly being a baby,
but still you want to be mad about such a thing
and you don't know what to be mad at.
Except the universe.

It was Jolly's voice when she
said that one word to Jilly.

Jilly she's having herself an afternoon
of doing wrong things at the rate of 1 per minute.
She turns on the stove knob and then
she puts the eggbeater in the toilet
and then she rips the 3-fish page
halfway across in Jeremy's book
and then she spills the Night Danger Red bottle
on the sofa and then
she aims her mother's ballpoint pen
in the light socket.
Mr. Jeremy he's mostly too busy to notice.

She also misuses Legos
by putting them up her nose and in the stove.

But it was one of those plastic tarantulas, black,
with all the long, bendy legs and great big smiley eyes,
they're sposed to hang in a car dangling down
and turning all around
bouncing to see the traffic.
I should have known.
Jolly should have known.
Mr. Jeremy himself should have known,
even being not even 3.

One minute Jilly's sitting on the floor all happy
talking in her language to the jungle spider,
and the next thing I know,
she's completely sputtering and waving her feet
in a fight with Jolly
who's trying to keep her from kicking—
You ever hear a baby coughing in a squeak not even their
own voice?

I was at a standstill.
Jilly's feet were punching everywhere,
and when her face came jerking around under Jolly's elbow
it was all red blotchy in a panic.
Jolly is bending over looking deep in her mouth
and then she turns Jilly over,
and she whacks her on her back, solid with her flat hand,
even with Jilly squirming in confusion
and making that squeak sound—
and then she turns her over frontwards,

pushes Jilly's shirt up out of the way,
she pushes on that little chest with her fingers,
but Jilly's fighting her with her hands all beating
everyplace Jolly touches this red baby.
Jolly's determined, she has such a face on her,
this is a war with whatever it is inside Jilly.
Jilly's sound is too bad to be true
and Jeremy he knows it and he stands completely still
on the floor.

Jolly she flips Jilly over and whacks her on her back
with her flat hand 4 times
then Jilly she almost flips over again
and Jolly pushes on her chest with 2 fingers 4 times too.
Then on her back 4 whacks, then on her chest 4 presses.
Jilly's turning color.

"Call 911," says Jolly in a voice
that could get the 911 people there already,
a voice nobody couldn't pay attention to.

Me, I'm going for the phone
and Jeremy's already there
and I see like a close-up of a movie,
he has the receiver up in his face
and he has his two fingers on the 9
and he pushes the button hard and lets it go just right
and I grab it and do the remaining pushing,
1 and 1 real fast.

Now Jilly's lips are going blue and black,
and Jolly has her flat on the floor

with her face completely asleep and her body—
you don't want to hear—it's so limp
it looks like this is the big one nobody planned for
and 911 answers
and I don't know what to say but
I tell them where
and I tell them who when they ask.
I tell them, "There's a baby, she's blue."
They pay attention real fast.

Jolly she's on the floor,
she has Jilly's chin up in her one hand,
and she's blowing into her nose and mouth both
while I'm talking
and then she has her fingers on Jilly's little fat arm up high
and she holds her fingers there
and she says, "There's a pulse but no breathing"
and she blows again
in Jilly's mouth and nose
and I say the same thing to the 911 phone,
"There's a pulse but no breathing." 911 says to me
is there a qualified CPR cardholder on the scene.
"No," I say. I don't think fast enough to understand.
Then I remember back to Jolly's homework
and brachial pulse.
And I go silent not knowing the answer
and I'm watching Jolly's head swinging back and forth slow, regular,
blowing into Jilly and then looking sideways at her chest.

Hurry, I tell the 911 phone, and I tell them again,
to speed them up.

911 says somebody is on their way, they'll be here soon
and I should hang on the phone
and listen to what they tell me.
Jolly's fingering Jilly's brachial pulse again
and this time she says "I can't find no pulse"
between her blowing into Jilly's nose and mouth.
I tell the 911 phone the same thing as Jolly says,
"She can't find no pulse,"
and they tell me they're gonna instruct me on the phone
and they begin saying we need to tilt the baby's head,
not too high
and open the airway
and do just exactly what Jolly's already doing.

But I tell them I didn't mean actually No back there
when they asked.
I say I meant Jolly didn't have her test yet, no card yet.
I tell them she's got her two fingers on the baby's chest
and she's pushing
and she's blowing in the baby's mouth and nose
like they must have done in her CPR class
where she goes to school.
The 911 phone tells me again the ambulance
is on their way and we should just hang on
and keep doing it.
Is there somebody can go outside and meet the paramedics,
they want to know from me.
I don't even know the answer to that one,
but I tell them Yes.

Jilly's too still.
Jeremy stares and grabs Jolly's arm and holds on.

Jolly she doesn't change what she's doing,
she's a machine now,
blow slow once, press Jilly's chest 5 times,
blow slow once, press 5 times,
it keeps going on
and you could scream with all the not knowing.

It's then Jolly says that word to Jilly, between blowing.
She says in a voice I never heard in her or anybody else,
a voice like an animal somewhere out in the dark
all reaching all alone,
she makes such a sound,
so clear I never heard a word so clear in my life,
or so soft,
"Breathe, Jilly."

There was sunshine coming in the window, and 911 was
talking on the phone
so I knew the world was going on,
and yet there was Jilly, like a stranger,
not even there.
Jolly kept blowing and pushing.
I kept wondering how it looked inside Jilly.
Was it complete dark?
And I never knew if Jilly ever heard her mother
say that word or not.

And it went on and it went on.
Jolly she didn't say anything again.
And the sound of her blowing into Jilly's nose and mouth
was all there was and it went on and on.

And the vomiting sound—
the puking,
the miracle shaking of Jilly's neck—
the throwup coming out and the spider leg
hurled up and out
and the vomit—real live human throwup—
and we all jumped and watched
and Jilly sputtered and screamed herself back into her life
and 911 kept saying, "Are you still there, are you still there?"

And I ran to meet the ambulance
down the stairs of course,
the elevator being broke like always.
There they were,
up they came running with me,
and their kits and their uniforms
and their voices.

And they took a look around
and started handling Jilly still screaming
and her mother sat there on the floor and put her finger
in a throwup puddle and felt it like you'd test the water.
One of them was finding Jilly's brachial pulse
and they were asking Jolly questions
and she was still there on her knees
with her one finger standing still in the puddle of throwup
and she answered them
and breathed hard, she was so tired.

I'm trying to explain to Jeremy
and hang on the phone
and explain to them what's happening

and I don't know how everything turns out
except Jilly's going to the hospital and Jolly too.
"She'll need a neuro check," says one of those paramedics,
and "We don't know she didn't aspirate something,"
says another,
and we all go out the door and down the stairs.
It happens like in somebody else's life because it's too much
for just one family of Jolly and her 2 kids,
a parade of 7 people going down the stairs,
one of them being carried still crying.

The siren made spectators,
now we're a show
with all their equipment
and Jolly walking along
with those eyes of hers
watching Jilly being lifted in the ambulance.
One of them puts out his hand to Jolly and she stares at it.
Then he waves it up,
"Come on," and she obeys it and gets in.
Jolly says something to Jeremy and me through the glass
but we don't know what it is
and I am in charge of Jeremy's disappointment
about not understanding any of this surprise event
of the day and they start the engine and begin to move.

64.

Jilly and Jolly are gone away in the ambulance.
Jeremy and me stand on the sidewalk holding hands
among the onlookers
who have got real interested in Jolly's life all of a sudden.

Mr. Jeremy is one confused person,
he hasn't got a clue about hospitals,
being that he doesn't remember being born.
"Jilly nap in truck"
is about as clear as he's gonna get for now.
I listen to the folks muttering Jeremy is a poor little kid
and his sister too,
and I don't believe them.

This comes as a surprise even to me, me not believing.
Maybe before, but not now.
How many of these neighbors
ignoring Jolly for her ignorance and bad luck
could go down on their knees
and save their kid from choking to death
this afternoon
while the world was going on outside in the sunshine?

Jeremy in his big deep glasses too. Not even 3 yet
and he punched the 9 on the phone.
He's pulling on my hand now,

he wants to run around the corner to see the ambulance
going on down the street.

"Jeremy, you did the 9 on the phone," I say to him,
pulling him in the opposite direction, away from the street.
"That was a real smart thing to do," I compliment him.
"Sure," he kicks a chicken bone from somebody's garbage.
"You did a good job," I tell him again.
"Sure. Leben over dere," he tells me.
I look where he's pointing.
Three dogs are nosing around the Dumpster,
one of them looks pregnant, all bulging and hanging.
"Three dogs," I say to Jeremy. "One Dumpster."

All at once I don't want to go back in Jolly's house.
It's not Jilly's throwup—
it's not that. I look down into Jeremy's tunnels to his eyes.
"Jilly nap in truck?" he asks me.
I tell him Yes. I think about what the paramedic said,
"They'll do a neuro check." And I'm thinking about Jolly,
how she held on and held on.

Back in Jolly's living room
I quick apply some soap and water to Jilly's throwup
and I scrub it with a towel
and I hang the whole mess up in about 5 minutes,
because me and Jeremy are getting out of here.

I quick call my Mom at the office
and I tell her Jeremy's coming to our house
probably to sleep over.
My Mom she says Sure

in her voice that's betting Jolly's done something stupid.
"We'll just be there, that's all," I tell my Mom,
and I'm on the edge of getting rude
so we say Good-bye.

We pack Jeremy a bag including his blanket and a truck
and 2 books,
and he says Sure he wants to see my house.
I explain Jilly gets to go to a great big hospital,
Jeremy he deserves a trip, too,
and we're gonna go on the bus
and he can help carry his clothes
in the grocery bag I found under the sink.

I leave a note for Jolly
so she'll know.

Mr. Jeremy tells 2 riders on the bus
all about Jilly threw up
and she's taking a nap in the truck
and Mommy hit her and blowed on her.
This isn't the way I'd tell it, but I sit there
listening to the 2 ladies admiring how straight he sits
like a good boy
and shaking their heads what a shame it is to hit a child.

Me, I'd tell how Jeremy pushed the 9 on the phone.
And I'd tell how Jolly never once stopped
doing what she was doing
to save her child from dying in front of her on the floor.
I sit on the bus holding Jeremy's clothes in the grocery bag
and I look at his legs swinging back and forth

hanging down from the seat
and I don't say anything
till it's time for him to get up and pull the cord for our stop.

65.

I show Jeremy where he gets to sleep
on the sofa, we put his blanket there
and we take out his truck and his 2 books he chose,
the one about the crab
and also the tool book that tells about shovels and wrenches.

And we tell my Mom how it happened.
"Tell my Mom what you did, Jeremy,"
I tell him down from where I'm sitting
on the conversation stool in the kitchen.
It's been the same stool
all the years I remember.
It's where I sat when I got her to say Yes I could sit for Jolly.
Jeremy's walking around
with my Mom's pan lid on his head.
"Jilly in truck," he tells my Mom,
looking important under his hat.

My Mom is poking potatoes with the kitchen fork
to bake them. I tell her,
"You know Jolly she had to take swimming with Jilly
and in the same period they had CPR classes,
and she had to do the brachial pulse
and the proper procedures all perfect,
she still hasn't had her test yet?"
My mother's attention is on this subject,
a potato is in her hand.

"Well, she just saved Jilly's life today," I tell my Mom,
"2 hours ago."
and I watch her face very careful.
She does the proper thing, instantly.
She praises Jolly. To me and to Jeremy.
"Your mommy she's a hero,"
she bends down to give him the news.
I tell her about the spider leg coming jumping out
in Jilly's throwup
and my Mom rolls her eyes and she praises Jolly again
and I go on giving her all the information,
about the blowing and the pressing,
and how Jeremy punched the 9 on the phone.

Now my Mom has discarded the potato and the fork
and she picks up Jeremy and whirls him around
and says how proud she is he's a hero too,
and I truly bite my tongue
not to get spiteful
about her getting spiteful before
about Jolly not taking hold.

66.

Sometimes the most real thing I remember
from that whole time
isn't Jolly's smelly sink drain
or her TV with no vertical hold
or how Jeremy learned to go in the toilet.
Not even that vomity spider leg
leaping up out of Jilly's mouth.
Sometimes the first scene that comes in my mind
isn't even the one about sitting in the bathtub with Jilly
covering each other's faces with soap designs
or that time
me and Jolly laughed so hard about the Vaseline
and Jilly crawled across the room.

Sometimes the first and foremost picture I remember
when I'm laying on my bed
looking at the ceiling crack
is the one of my mother
whirling Jeremy around in the kitchen
and she's telling him he's a hero
and explaining he had presence of mind,
her words, how he punched the 9 like a good big boy
and he helped save his sister's life.

Even all these months later,
when Jolly never calls me ever anymore.

She has a babysitting pool now
with a Moms Up girl named Caroline,
who has 2 kids also. They exchange.
I see Jolly sometimes in B Hallway,
she's counting down the credits to get finished with school,
she ain't—she hasn't—got too many left to go.
She's doing practice interviews for jobs.
And there was a picture of her and Jilly in the school paper,
it said STUDENT SAVES OWN CHILD.
And in smaller letters it said,
Credits Moms Up CPR Class for Skills.
And—

It's all completely different now.
I been broken off,
like part of her bad past.
I was the one that knew the saddest parts of Jolly, I guess.

I do some babysitting sometimes
for other people—
And I got a job cleaning a part of a church
with Myrtle and Annie
on Tuesday and Thursday and Saturday.

One time Jolly in B Hallway
poked me very obvious,
that old look of the lights going on in her eyes for a minute:
"Hey, you wouldn't guess what come up out of that dirt."
She poked me.

I looked at her and my heart was so stretching,
like a room wanting company to come in,

I got all excited with her poking me,
I even forgot which dirt she meant.
I even looked blank at her, probably, I was so knocked over
hearing her voice all eager,
reminding me of the good times we used to have
in her dirty, ignorant house.
"Huh?" I said, wanting to laugh at some joke with her.
Any joke would have done.

"We got a little green thing,
a little lemon thing comin' up," she said. "Bye," she said.
And she went on down B Hallway,
carrying her spiral notebook in her arm.

And it's kind of strange
that of all the pictures I might remember,
from that whole time,
sometimes it's only Jeremy up high in my mother's kitchen.
I look up there where he's swinging round and round
and there's his pants too short
and his socks not matching,
plus one of them slid down into his shoe
and his shirt's all tore at the neck.
And I wonder how it would be for Jeremy
in another place,
even in another time
where he'd have new clothes
that would go together in their colors and a dad.

But here he is now, this Jeremy,
laughing in his voice I know so close,
I think he's forgot the fear and all the hardness

for a moment. Here he is
a cheerful child
a boy in the air
ready for his dinner,
in his forgetful joy he's laughing down at my Mom
who's looking up there to him,
her mouth wide open and full of praise.

About This Point Signature Author

VIRGINIA EUWER WOLFF has written two other books for young adults, *The Mozart Season* and *Probably Still Nick Swansen*. When asked where she got the idea for *Make Lemonade*, Jinny Wolff says, "When I was a young mother, I had to put my babies in an old plastic-upholstered high chair from the Salvation Army that I could never get clean. It completely overwhelmed me at the time — even now I could pick it out from a million others. Jolly, Jilly, and Jeremy came straight out of that dirty high chair."

Virginia Euwer Wolff lives in Oregon City, Oregon.